A BAD DAY IN HEAVEN

"You're screwing up every case so far," Gabriel said. "Divorced! Irretrievable marital breakdown. Marriage annulled. Irreconcilable sexual disharmony. I mean what is happening?"

"We had a bad run," said Jackson.

"A bad run? Seventy-two consecutive failures!"

"Men and women have changed. They're not like they used to be," said O'Reilly.

"Well things have changed up here as well. I'm getting pressure. From above, okay? They say our department's a lost cause." He threw O'Reilly the last file. "It's a tough one but you'll have to crack it. If you don't—you don't come back."

"Gabriel, you cannot do this to us." But of course, they knew he could.

"That's the new incentive scheme. You're mission is to unite a man and a woman. When you've done that, you come back. If you fail, you stay down there forever."

"The rules suck," said Jackson.

"The whole thing sucks," said O'Reilly, but it was not clear whether she was talking about the mission, the rules, or perhaps, quite simply, the entire universe.

"It's out of my hands," said Gabriel, "If I were you," he concluded, "I would commence with the female."

A LIFE
LESS
ORDINARY

~

A Novel by

John Hodge

A SIGNET BOOK

For Lucy

SIGNET
Published by the Penguin Group
Penguin Putnam Inc., 375 Hudson Street,
New York, New York 10014, U.S.A.
Penguin Books Ltd, 27 Wrights Lane,
London W8 5TZ, England
Penguin Books Australia Ltd, Ringwood,
Victoria, Australia
Penguin Books Canada Ltd, 10 Alcorn Avenue,
Toronto, Ontario, Canada M4V 3B2
Penguin Books (N.Z.) Ltd, 182–190 Wairau Road,
Auckland 10, New Zealand

Penguin Books Ltd, Registered Offices:
Harmondsworth, Middlesex, England

First published by Signet, an imprint of Dutton Signet,
a member of Penguin Putnam Inc.

First Printing, October, 1997
10 9 8 7 6 5 4 3 2 1

 REGISTERED TRADEMARK—MARCA REGISTRADA

Printed in the United States of America

1

Mayhew heard the gun and knew that he was alive.

He ran a clutch of stubby fingers through his hair, clearing a few fragments of apple from his scalp. Always the same sequence—dismay at her request to play this game, fatal resignation as the hour approached, terror as he placed the apple on his head, and then a flurry of questions in his mind: Was she concentrating? Had she been drinking? Was there a strong wind, or a speck of dust in her eye? A fault in the sight, or a piece of grit in the barrel? Was there anything different about today, any trivial glitch, any insignificant error, that could redirect the bullet one inch lower so that it penetrated his skull and scattered his brain across the expensively marbled terrazzo?

Each time, as he prepared to die, he would recognize the tremor from the disintegrating apple, which preceded, by an instant, the crack of the gun, for bullets travel faster than sound. And with that he knew he was alive, and would wonder why he had ever been concerned, since he knew that his employer's daughter, Ms. Celine Naville, twenty-four years old, rich, bored, and beautiful, was truly an excellent shot.

They stood for a moment. No sound disturbed the silent heat of the day. Sunlight sparkled off the surface of the pool that lay between them. Celine smiled as Mayhew moved his limbs, as though he were discovering anew the joys of life. With a bow, he departed, moving toward the cool interior of the house. She was alone, and as she opened the chamber, and the single brass casing, still smoking, tumbled to the ground, Celine felt, for just one second, that her life was complete.

2

The man was an institution. No one knew how long he had been hanging around the precinct, but it seemed like forever, certainly for as long as Jackson and O'Reilly had been assigned there and how long was that? One hundred years, or one hundred and fifty? No one was counting. At first the guy had irritated Jackson and he wondered why no one ever booked him for panhandling or aggravation, but as time went by, Jackson mellowed, taking comfort in the man's familiar presence and his one story, repeated over and over and over again, to any soul who would listen and many who would not.

"We're in the garden, right, and this guy, you know, says, 'Whatever you want,' okay? 'Whatever you want. Except that one tree. The fruit of that tree you do not eat.' He's totally clear on this. I got no problem. He goes inside to make a phone call and what does she do? What does she do? She eats the apple. I can't believe what I'm seeing. He says, 'Don't eat.' She eats. What can I do? It's unbelievable. And since then, it's like it's, I don't know, it's like it's all gone wrong."

And then he started crying. This too was a familiar part of his routine.

Jackson and O'Reilly watched in silence as he moved away toward a group of patrolmen who laughed at him as he told his story once again.

"Poor guy," said Jackson.

O'Reilly said nothing.

"I think he lost his mind," said Jackson. A conversational offer: But O'Reilly was not interested. She was annoyed at Gabriel for keeping them waiting for so long, sitting out in the squad room surrounded by all the fuck-ups, whores, adulterers, sinners, and betrayers, each one packing a stack of excuses and a smart-talking, white-clad lawyer. And she was annoyed at Jackson for not being sympathetic to her general state of annoyance about everything else. The man had a good nature, but surely, she felt, there had to be a limit.

Gabriel emerged from his office and beckoned them in. O'Reilly had harbored a lot of concern about this meeting and one look at her superior's worn, ugly face told her that she was right to do so. She and Gabriel had, at one time, enjoyed a certain domestic understanding, and she more than anyone was sensitive to his moods and alert to the maelstrom of savage politics that swirled around him.

He didn't waste time. Before they even sat down, he was prowling around, a tortured bundle of barely suppressed rage.

"I don't know what you're doing, but you're doing it wrong," he told them. "You're screwing up every fucking case so far as I can tell."

A stack of files stood on his desk. One by one he lifted them before dropping each one to the floor.

"Look at these. Divorced! Divorced! Divorced! Irretrievable marital breakdown. Marriage annulled. Irreconcilable sexual disharmony. I mean what is happening?"

Jackson and O'Reilly shifted in their seats.

"Talk to me!"

"We had a bad run," said Jackson.

"A bad run! A bad run! How bad? Seventy-two consecutive failures. That bad?"

"Men and women have changed. They're not like they used to be," said O'Reilly.

"Well, things have changed up here as well," and he softened for a moment, which worried O'Reilly even more.

"You see," continued Gabriel, "I'm getting pressure. From *above*, okay? You know what I'm talking about. There are some—I won't name them—close to the center of power, who have openly expressed doubt as to the worth of our entire department. They say it's a lost cause."

"They can't believe that."

"Jackson, I'm just telling you like it is. We're under review. In the meantime, I am instructed to introduce a new incentive scheme for our leading operatives."

Gabriel's manner had switched back, and O'Reilly sensed the distance opening up between them, the distance between headquarters and the front line, between cause and effect.

"Leading operatives?" she inquired.

"That's you," said Gabriel, uncomfortable in delivering a compliment.

"Skip the flattery: Where's the beef?"

Gabriel looked at her. A cold hard woman. He thought, as he always did, of the tragedy that had brought her to this condition and tried to imagine her as she must once have been. But she was right, there was no need for flattery. Theirs was a relationship founded on respect and respect knows only the truth.

He threw her the last file. "It's a tough one, but you'll crack it. And if you don't—"

He could feel their attention.

"If you don't—you don't come back."

Jackson was first off the block.

"You cannot be serious, Gabriel. You cannot do this to us. You owe us. You cannot do this."

But they knew he could.

"That's the new incentive scheme. Your mission is to unite a man and a woman. Blah blah blah. When you've done that, you come back. If you fail, you stay down there forever."

"Special powers?" asked Jackson.

"No special powers. You know the rules. You go to earth, you're pretty much like everybody else. You just last longer."

"The rules suck," said Jackson.

"The whole thing sucks," said O'Reilly, but it was not clear whether she was talking about the mission, the rules, or perhaps quite simply the entire universe.

"I hate it down there," said Jackson, defeat in his voice. "I really hate it."

A memory flashed through his mind. It was a memory of pain and anguish.

"It's out of my hands," said Gabriel. *"Liberatum mane."*

Jackson and O'Reilly were silent.

"If I were you," he concluded, "I would commence with the female."

3

"**S**he is the secret daughter of Marilyn Monroe and John F. Kennedy, right? That's why Marilyn was murdered by barbiturate injection, within hours of the girl's birth, okay?"

America had not yet been outstandingly kind to Robert Lewis; nor yet had it been outstandingly cruel. Arriving as a tourist at the age of twenty-four and staying as an illegal immigrant for nearly two years now, he had enjoyed its climate, its outsize burgers, its panoramic anonymity, and the open, friendly manner of its people. Still more did he enjoy the open, friendly manner of his American girlfriend, Lily, with whose radiant, well-nourished smile and cheerleader legs he had been living these last twelve months. They had been blissfully happy together and he foresaw a glorious future. Once married to her, he would attain citizenship, and then he could truly begin to exploit the many opportunities that awaited a dynamic young man in this mighty nation. If, at the moment, she worked

in a bar and he as a janitor at the corporate headquarters of Naville Industrial Holdings, then what
of it? At least they were happy. Besides which, the
route to his fortune was clearly mapped: He intended to write a novel.

"Okay, so the girl grows up in an orphanage in
Wichita, unaware of her incredible parentage."

Ted and Frank listened carefully. In the humid
dungeon of the janitors' storeroom, lesser men
would have given in to the urge to sleep, but Ted
and Frank resisted. They had worked at Naville
Holdings for many years and had watched the arrival of many young janitors like Robert, all full of
hope, and had watched them depart, broken by the
tedium of labor. They had listened to a steady
stream of pitches for novels, screenplays, sex aids,
arcade games, and automotive designs that would
change the world, but none of them did. And so
they listened to Robert with the indulgence and
courtesy of those who know that all dreams must
soon be crushed.

"Years go by," Robert continued. "College. Uni-
versity. She's smart, she's successful, she's beautiful."

"Then what?" asked Ted.

"Well then, then she goes into politics and gets
sent to London, England, as U.S. ambassador."

Frank took this in and nodded. "Let me guess,"
he said. "She goes to London, where she unravels
first of all the mystery of her own identity and also
the secret of the Nazi gold hidden underneath the
embassy by her secret grandfather, old Joe Kennedy."

"Uh. Yeah," said Robert, "as a matter of fact, that's more or less exactly what happens."

Frank and Ted, connoisseurs of frustrated ambition, let him down gently.

"It's kind of obvious, Robert," said Ted.

"Of course, it's obvious," said Robert, defending desperately. "It's a trash novel. You buy it at the airport, you take it on holiday. It's a winner, guys, a best-seller. One year from now you'll be saying, yeah, we remember Robert, his dream came true."

The two older men were spared from their obligation to respond by the sudden opening of the storeroom door and a chilling blast of cold air that enveloped them all. Robert, his back to the door, did not need to turn around. In his colleagues' eyes, he saw fear, fear that could be generated only by a woman, one woman: Violet Eldred Gesteten.

Violet Eldred Gesteten's great-great-grandmother had engaged in cannibalism in order to survive a harrowing snowbound pioneer's journey across the Rocky Mountains. Her great-grandmother had survived the sinking of the *Titanic*. Her grandmother had led a brief but violent Marxist revolt among unemployed Pennsylvania steel workers during the Great Depression, and her mother had kicked ass in Chicago, 1968.

The current representative of the genetic line was, if anything, tougher than her female antecedents. To make matters worse, she was confined in a less exciting, less violent world. As Chief Supervisor (Hygiene and Cleansing) within the corporate base, she ruled with a will of iron, a tongue of fire, and a heart of stone, all reinforced with a small but perfectly fitting knuckleduster, which she had inherited from her Marxist grandmother, along with the will to use it.

Frank and Ted immediately leaped toward their trays of dusters, cloths, and polishes, but it was not for them that Violet Eldred had come. Her basilisk gaze settled on Robert as he turned to face her, rising from his chair.

"Ms. Gesteten," he stammered, "what a—what a pleasant surprise."

She said nothing.

"I'd love to stay and talk. Really I would. But we have work to get on with."

He went to pass her, but a single finger on his chest arrested his progress. With her other hand she reached inside her jacket.

Fearing the appearance of the knuckleduster or a blade of some description, Frank and Ted were relieved when she produced only an envelope, evidently destined for Robert.

He took the envelope and pulled it open. From within he took the short, brutal letter. He read it quickly.

"Robots!" he exclaimed with unexpected vigor. "You're trying to tell me that I'm going to be replaced with a robot, that a robot is going to get down on its little robot hands and knees and clean the dirt from every corner of every office? I think not, Ms. Gesteten!"

"At least the robot won't spend its time trying to write a trash novel."

As her eyes bored into his, Robert knew he had no secrets from this woman.

"I see," he said, "it's personal."

"Nothing to do with me, Robert," she replied. "This comes right from the top, from Mr. Naville himself. He wants increased efficiency and less corporate fat all the way down. And you are corporate fat."

A flicker of rebellion still burned in Robert's heart. After all, was this how America treated its founding fathers? Was this how the land of the free welcomed the teeming millions? Surely a simple appeal to justice would secure a reprieve.

"Okay," he said, "maybe it's about time I paid a visit to Mr. Naville."

"It's too late, Robert," said Ms. Gesteten, as a sour parody of a smile twisted its way across her face like a sidewinder across a desert. "You're fired."

4

Elliot Zweikel's downfall, inevitably, was his inability to distinguish between bravado and bravery. It was a deficiency he would live to regret, but only just.

Paying a visit to Celine was always a pleasure for Elliot, and it was with a confident anticipatory air that he swept past the gate security and up toward the mansion in his Porsche that afternoon. He enjoyed their gutsy sparing and the little games of cat-and-mouse that heightened his sexual appetite for this already alluring woman. For years he had, as he saw it, worked hard to prepare her for the role of his life's principal companion. Not his only companion, of course—no, that would be absurd—but certainly his most frequent. The public face of his private life. God, he had worked hard. When they first met, it was all there, the raw material that made her so perfect: the beauty, the wealth, the cool disdain, but like a block of marble she still required sculpting. And boy, had he sculpted.

17

In the absence of a mother (lost in a bottle some-where), and a father (devoted to his dollars), Celine knew nothing of social skills, had no conversation-level knowledge of art, wine, or politics, and was prone to blurt out the truth about other people's second-rate cosmetic surgery at inappropriate moments.

Under his guidance, Pygmalion-like, she had blossomed into the region's most desirable flower. On matters emotional-sexual, as he thought of it, she also owed him a debt. A short string of dumb studs and college kids with Ferraris had left her with little knowledge of the demands, routines, debits and credits of true Practical Relationship Management, or "love," as she had once referred to it in the early days, with the naïveté that had been her hallmark. It was a character trait whose passing he did not mourn: All those crying fits, slammed telephones, threats to leave, possessive grasping, and pseudo suicides. What a drag. All that non-sense was behind them now, thank God, and wasn't she a fitter, more useful woman as a result? But it had all been effort. And that was before you even counted the work he had put into her teeth.

The only cloud in the sky was a nagging worry that perhaps he had improved her too much, if such a thing was possible, that she had grown too confi-dent, too knowing, too resilient. As he walked through the house, past the four Vermeer portraits and the two Picassos, Elliot tried to recall what hap-pened at the end of *My Fair Lady*. Didn't Audrey Hepburn go off with some young punk? Freddie? Some stud with a Ferrari? More or less. Make a man sick, that kind of thing, after all that Rex Harrison had done for her. Still, that was just a movie: Real life was different. He paused at the French windows and wondered, "Have I treated her too well?"

It was a sobering thought. In Elliot's experience, gratitude did not come naturally to women. Mostly they were unable to express it for being treated well; only for being treated less badly than they might have been. Surely he had treated her badly enough? The weight of evidence—affairs, absences, substance abuse—all shouted Yes, so why had she declined to marry him? He ran over the scene from the night before: French restaurant, wine, candles, smart conversation, a little bit of off-court tennis coaching, some trivial but costly platinum jewelry, and bang, No. What the fuck was going on? It made no sense. Had she lost it, gone insane? The alternative, rearing up in front of Elliot, was far more disturbing: that she was expressing her own will. But as swiftly as he rejected the notion, Elliot knew it was so. The bitch. Still the game was not over and the advantage lay, as always, with experience.

As Elliot left the house and walked into the late afternoon sun, he saw across the pool another irritating example of Celine's new "will," the red bulbous apple perched on top of Mayhew's head, shattering at the crack of the gun. It was not that he objected to the use and ownership of weaponry, far from it, or that he feared for the life of Mayhew, once again, far from it. In fact, a bullet between the eyes of the frosty English jerk would be a welcome development from Elliot's viewpoint; it was more to do with its symbolism: personal achievement, skill, risk-taking, and confidence. What did these amount to, if not independence?

"Nice trick, Celine," he said.

Celine did not even turn around, showed no flicker of surprise at his presence. He was a pest. He had spoiled her moment of elation.

"Do you want to try your luck?" she asked as she opened the chamber and the scent of cordite teased at her nostrils. Still she did not look at him.

"With the gun?" asked Elliot, almost hoping for a shot at Mayhew.

"With the fruit."

"I have no time for games, Celine," said Elliot, scanning the terrace. Not bad. Not bad at all for the environs of the super rich. Almost tasteful. Of course, he would change a few things once the old man went to heaven. Get rid of that fucking butler for a start. Who did he think he was, staring at him like he was a piece of dog shit? Your days are numbered, buddy.

"Elliot." It was Celine. "If you are afraid, why not just say so?"

She was lying down now in the shade. He was standing in the sun. She was throwing him bait, but, no, he would not rise.

"Last night, we discussed a certain proposal."

"And I said no, because you cheat, Elliot."

"Okay, I am flirtatious. It's in my nature. But think carefully—do you have any idea how difficult it is for a woman to find a good husband in this town? Or a good dentist for that matter?"

If Celine was listening, she showed no sign of it.

Undeterred, Elliot came to the point. "Celine—I am serious."

At first it seemed that, indeed, she had not been listening. Perhaps behind those impenetrable shades she was asleep. No sound, no movement. Mayhew squinted and pursed his lips. A small bead of sweat formed on Elliot's forehead. He waited. Celine reached to a bowl of fruit that lay beside her. She lifted an apple and threw it toward Elliot. Instinctively he caught it and immediately wished that he had not. He knew what was coming.

"Serious, Elliot? How serious?"

Clearly he had treated her too well. It was all so obvious now. This is where it had all been leading: her "will," her confidence, resilience, the whole damn thing. Well, fuck her. He would show her. If the butler could do it, so could he. No problem at all. And afterward, hell, she would see just how desperate things can get for a woman.

He placed the apple on his head.

Celine was surprised, impressed even. She had Elliot figured for a coward—a swaggering, charismatic, bullying coward. But this was something new, for she did not underestimate the bravery involved every time that Mayhew played her game. Mayhew was, however, as Celine was well aware, a man steeped in the pointless and violent initiation rituals of ancient British regiments, a man for whom the fear of imminent death at the hands of a spoiled young woman was tempered by the solid bravery that had forged an empire.

Was it now so for Elliot?

The prospect was intriguing and she watched him closely as she loaded the gun. He stood still, his breathing shallow, eyes closed, but that bead of sweat was now a torrent.

"Are you ready?" she asked, her words dropping dead in the flat, hot air between them.

Elliot grimaced, but said nothing.

She watched him again, looking for signs of indecision, of regret, of cowardice. But apart from the sweating, which she had to concede was appropriate, he seemed determined to go ahead.

"If you move, my answer is no."

"Celine, are you sure this is wise?" he said suddenly as his life flashed before him and he saw himself as a little boy playing in the front room in dappled sunlight, with a loving mother, and nothing ahead now but darkness and he wanted to scream, I don't want to die. But he didn't. He just said, "Celine, are you sure this is wise?"

It was too late now. Celine was taking aim.

"Don't talk," she said, "it puts me off."

But as her finger curled around the trigger and squeezed to begin the detonation, Elliot had second thoughts. This, he realized precisely at the same moment as Celine (and it was the only time in their entire relationship when they shared the same thought), this was not bravery.

This was the other thing.

"Stop!" he shouted as his arm swung up, a pointless and involuntary movement. Stop, he might have cried, with all his voice, but the bullet was already on its way.

The apple was unharmed.

From the moment he hit the marble, it was clear he was not dead. Wounded certainly, perhaps even mortally, but he was not dead yet. Blood spurted from his head through a small hole about an inch above his left eye, and as he underwent a seizure, the blood scattered and sprayed into the pool. Celine looked down at him, disappointed in his cowardice, but relieved by the clear validation of her previous assessment.

"Mayhew, would you call for a doctor?"

Mayhew also looked down at Elliot, writhing in his own blood. He had seen plenty of men shot through the head. Shot a few of them himself, as a matter of fact. He fancied he could see some of Elliot's brain peeping through the entry wound, but saw no need to point that out to Miss Celine. After all, he was only the butler.

"My pleasure, madam," he said with the discreet fractional bow of his head that so endeared him to his employer.

5

The knife of destiny spun on the dark old pine. Many lives had been guided by the knife, many decisions made. All that you needed to do was to draw your circle in chalk, divide it in two, and label the halves. Whatever issue you liked, it made no difference. The knife did not distinguish between matters trivial and mortal. Constructed from strange metals, shaped and sharpened by hands more powerful than our own, handed down through generation after generation, not as a possession but as owner of those who held it, the knife had existed always, would exist always, and could not be questioned.

Al watched it spin. As present guardian of the knife, Al, by now a man worn older than his forty years, had come to see life as nothing more than a series of choices, although, like all guardians, he did not use the knife himself. Good and bad, life and death, ketchup and mustard, all were nothing more than two halves of a circle to Al. Since he had opened his bar and diner some eighteen years earlier, he had acquired a large, loyal clientele, many of whom he had coaxed with the aid of the knife through the successive crises of youth and adulthood. Robert was one such. Although he had only been a regular presence here for about a year, he had used the blade on a number of occasions, principally for trivial matters, as on this occasion when he demanded of the knife: whiskey or beer?

The blade slowed gracefully to a halt.

"Whiskey please, Al," said Robert.

"Alcohol will not solve your problems. All it will do is cause them to recede behind a misleading haze of impaired consciousness," said Al as he dropped the knife back in its case.

"Better make that a double, then," said Robert. It was not that he was ungrateful for the barman's advice or that he doubted its wisdom, it was simply that there are times for reality and times for oblivion, and Robert had not walked six blocks in sweltering head-breaking heat to Al's Bar in search of reality. Being fired was an unpleasant experience and hardly one that he cared to dwell on. After the sadistic rapier thrusts of Ms. Gesteten's interpersonal manner, his dignity had been dented still further by an unseemly scuffle with the security staff. His ejection from the buildings via the fire exit was worryingly heavy with symbolism. It was not that he particularly enjoyed or treasured his job, but its loss did not bode well. Was this the end of his relationship with American capitalism? Was this how he would leave America? Shoved, lifted, and kicked out of the back door without any concern for his welfare, was this a taste of his future?

It was these thoughts, and the need to soothe

them with two particularly potent balms that drove him to Al's Bar, where the knife selected the first. As he trickled the whiskey down the back of his throat, his eyes scanned the bar for the second. There, in one corner, serving two executive types their smoked chicken salad and mineral water, was the svelte shapely smiling form of Lily. A second wave of warmth spread through Robert as he watched her and his troubles seemed to recede in a way not even alcohol could contrive. Lily was truly succour to a troubled soul, a timely reminder that he was not some drifting loser, but a man of charisma, of potential, of a certain rough-hewn physical charm, and he reflected that with Lily on his arm, minor setbacks such as losing his job could be filed under *N* for "no big deal," or better still "new opportunity."

"Robert, what are you doing here at this time of day?" she asked as he approached. Her welcome was perhaps a little less rapturous than Robert had envisaged, but then, this was the busiest time of day and she had no inkling of his recent employment-related, negative life-experience.

"Lily"—he could not help himself,—"I'm so glad to see you."

But Lily did not respond in the same fashion.

"Answer me. You're supposed to be at work."

Now Robert decided was the time to tell her. He had planned to wait until that evening, perhaps in bed, when he would tell her of his plan to go full time as a novelist working from home and, of course, unpaid at first. But clearly there was a misunderstanding here. She thought he was AWOL from work, the kind of idleness which as an all-

American girl, steeped in work ethic, she could not tolerate. It was his fault; he would clarify the situation.

"Lily, I got bad news."

"Oh God, what kind of bad news?" A frown creased her perfect brow and her full lips pouted with concern as she took his hand in hers.

This, felt Robert, was more like it.

"Lily—I—" He prepared himself for the full onslaught of her sympathy. She would hold him, caress him, smother him with hot passionate uninhibited kisses. At this moment of crisis they would reaffirm their togetherness. It would not be a surprise if they needed to go through to Al's back room for a spot of impromptu sexual healing.

"I got fired."

She dropped his hand like nuclear waste. The frown deepened and her lips contorted into something that, on any other woman, Robert would have called a sneer.

"That kind of bad news," she said.

This was not going according to plan. At this rate it seemed highly unlikely that Al's back room or even their own bedroom would see any sexual healing today, impromptu or even heavily negotiated and discounted, as was her habit, against future favors. Alarm bells were beginning to sound in Robert's head, but still he blamed himself. He had not explained the full circumstances.

"They replaced me with a robot."

"Yeah? Well I know how they feel."

The alarms were deafening now. This was all wrong. This was not the script that Robert had so carefully prepared, this was not a sultry midafternoon seduction in which raw physical energy defined what it was to be alive and spat with contempt at the drab inert world of jobs and sackings. This was an altogether different unacceptable scenario, one that he could not understand.

"Huh?" he said, frozen in the headlights as she accelerated toward him, foot to the floor, stereo turned to full volume playing, playing a familiar tune.

"I've been meaning to tell you for a while, and now seems as good a time as any. Robert, I am leaving you."

And with such casual brevity did she crush her lover, now ex, into the asphalt.

"Leaving me? You? Leaving me? What are you talking about?"

He was attracting a small crowd now. "We never discussed you leaving me; we never planned that. We planned an apartment in New York, a ranch in Montana, a ski lodge in Vermont, but we never planned you leaving."

"Robert," she commanded, a sharpness in her voice as he was silenced, "now listen."

She began to reveal, and with each revelation his despair multiplied, squared, cubed, went binary, logarithmic, exponential, universal.

"His name is Ryan," she began. "He teaches aerobics. We're in love. And we are going to Miami."

That was it. That was the song. He should have known. For the last two months she had been playing "Physical" by Olivia Newton-John on the CD player at least three times every evening. It was all so clear now. Aerobics. Ryan. Love. Miami. Physical. "Lily, how can you do this to me? At a time like this?" said Robert, sniveling through a curtain of tears. He fell to his knees and grasped hopelessly at the hem of her skirt. Displays of emotion were not his forte, but he had recently read a self-improvement text berating Men for Bottling Up Their Feelings and Thus Inhibiting Communication, which was judged to be Important in Relationships, and so he threw himself into this role of bereavement with all the gusto he could muster.

"Don't leave me Lily, don't leave me."

"I want a man," she said, "not a dreamer."

Clearly, self-abasement was not working. Rapidly reviewing the text in his mind, Robert remembered that what Women really Admire is Positive, Can-Do Capability at a time when so many Men are Underachieving Slobs. Acting on this, he sprang to his feet.

"Lily, we can talk about this. I'll get another job. We can put things back together."

"Sorry, Robert, but as of tonight, you are going home alone." And that was that.

The knife had spun for Robert many times by nightfall and had indicated beer and whiskey with equal favor. His thoughts and memories had become more and more confused, until it seemed he had been in the bar for centuries, living off the memories of a single day: rewinding, replaying, editing, seeking patterns in the chaos, clutching at fragments of meaning before they slipped through his fingers.

Al had serviced Robert's requirements for oblivion. He had advised restraint, but did not impose it. The customer was king. Of Lily there had been no further sign. She had walked from the bar and was already fading from Robert's mind. He struggled to compose a mental image of her, starting methodically from her immaculate pedicure and ending at her lustrous brown hair, but with each pass there were areas of increasing vagueness, sections of anatomy that he was forced to hazard a guess at, or fill in with generic memories of other women of his bodily and photographic acquaintance. He took out a few snapshots of Lily from his wallet, hoping to revive his memory, but he fumbled and they fell to the floor and although he searched for nearly an hour, he did not find them; they were lost.

Later, at home, their home as once it had been, a small one-bedroom apartment in a modern development, it was clear that Lily would not be coming back. All her things, and some of his—the Walkman, the blender, his leather jacket—were gone, as were all the photographs. Now he could remember almost nothing of what she looked like, as though they had never met. All that remained was her voice, and even that was merging with those other voices of the day: with Frank and Ted, and Ms. Gesteten, all coalescing into one composite accusatory voice that haunted him as he collapsed fully clothed on the bed.

Kind of obvious, Robert.

You're fired.

We're in love.

We're going to Miami.

You're fired.

You're fired.

You're fired.

At first it was a blur. A montage of colors and a meaningless babble of sounds. Gradually the colors grouped into images and the images sharpened into figures. The sounds took on pitch, wave form, and volume, and became almost recognizable. But still all was meaningless. However, even as he searched for meaning, he began to experience a threat, for it seemed, in a way that could not be explained, that his life was in danger. Here in this incomprehensible baffling world, surrounded by people he did not know and rules he could not learn, he was about to die. Fear grew and gripped him and just when it seemed he would either understand or die, the figures dissolved again into shapes and colors and the words into incoherent sounds. Just before the final fading of all sound and image, Robert was aware of a feeling of salvation. His life, it seemed, was no longer in danger and he was just aware, deep in his sleep, of relief from fear and of some awesome overpowering force that heralded this relief. And then, as sunlight poured through the window, he awoke to the beat of a harsh rhythmic knocking.

6

Jackson knocked at the door until his fist hurt. He was still getting used to it. He and O'Reilly had been down here for about four months and the endless, bizarre, and revolting sensations that a body could undergo were still a surprise to him. Every day there was something new, some fresh indignity imposed upon him by the rules of biology. O'Reilly did not share his distaste and seemed to take some perverse masochistic delight in eating, pissing, shitting, farting, belching, and all those other ugly accompaniments of life that he found so repulsive. And then there was pain. Pain, so as far as Jackson could tell, was endless. Every time you walked into something, or hit your shin, or stood up too quickly and hit a shelf with your head, you got pain. Why? There was no reason. Jackson had once submitted a written complaint about pain, but Gabriel had refused even to pass it on, warning Jackson not to meddle. So pain lived on. One month after they came down, for instance, Jackson developed a toothache. There was no reason for it that he could find, he couldn't see how it advanced His purpose or anyone else's for he, Jackson, to have a toothache. But after several days of total pain, he was faced with a choice: either spend from their limited allowance on expensive but qualified dental care or let O'Reilly assault him with a pair of heated pliers. Jackson did not consider this a difficult decision, but before he could reach the dentist's chair, his partner had trapped him in a washroom and performed a merciless and bloody extraction.

Their relationship had been a little strained since then, and the surveillance of their subjects had been conducted largely in silence.

For a long time it had seemed that nothing was going to happen, that the chosen man and the chosen woman were locked inside impenetrable and mutually exclusive worlds, each with its own supposedly stable relationship. The days dragged by and the weeks were unending, watching these couples go through their farcical and pointless dance without any prospect of a finish. Hour after hour was spent sitting in cars, eavesdropping through headphones to arguments and the sexual grunts that followed. This was what passed for reconnaissance and planning. There seemed no way forward and no way out. Perhaps, Jackson feared, this was it. Perhaps they faced an eternity on earth, an eternity of pain. But lately, things had begun to roll a little. The smooth rhythms of their subjects' bad matches had been disrupted by strife and by truth. The impenetrable worlds had begun to weaken a little. Unmistakably now, there was a hint of chaos in the air. Jackson could sense it and started to wonder just what forces controlled such events. Where did chaos come from? Were chaos and fate working together? He had tried to discuss it with O'Reilly, but she was a hard woman and little given to whimsical speculation.

"O'Reilly," he asked her one morning, "do you ever wonder?"

"Nope," she replied.

And that was the end of it.

So when at last, they found themselves at Robert's door, Jackson could not suppress the first beat of hope that soon their mission might be complete and they might leave this blighted earth. With enthusiasm then, he knocked at the door until his fist hurt.

Inside, as the knocking ceased and Robert remembered that he was alone, he stumbled to the door, echoes of his dream still reverberating in his head. Confronting him as he opened it were a man and a woman. The man was a tall, broad-shouldered African American with graying hair and a waistline that threatened expansion. The woman was small, white, and wiry, her hair tied back and her starched white blouse rising up her throat. Both wore heavy raincoats inappropriate to the season and fashion, but somehow fitting to their demeanor.

"Mr. Lewis? Mr. Robert Lewis?" said the man.

"Yes," said Robert, "that's me."

"My name is Jackson," said the man, "and this is my associate Ms. O'Reilly."

Robert nodded politely. O'Reilly looked at him blankly.

Jackson continued. "We are from the Firm But Fair Collection and Eviction Agency." He handed Robert a business card bearing that legend and produced a sheaf of typed papers.

"Now I have list of certain items that we are empowered to collect under federal and state law in lieu of unpaid debts. Now I could read you the list, but frankly it's just the entire contents of your apartment."

Robert was stunned. Debts? He knew of no debts.

Jackson could see his turmoil and paused for a moment but O'Reilly, more focused, prompted him. "Jackson."

"Furthermore, we are contracted to serve upon you a notice of eviction from these premises forthwith."

"I beg your pardon?" said Robert.

"One year of unpaid rent, mac," said O'Reilly.

Robert looked from one to the other. He could make no sense of this. Unpaid rent?

"No, no, you see," he told them, "it's all right. There has been a mistake. I don't owe any rent. I gave my girlfriend the money to pay the . . ."

His voice trailed away as he discovered a new level of betrayal. In his head he could hear the refrain of her aerobic theme tune.

Jackson sensed the young man's dismay, and almost felt like crying to see such honest devotion spurned. "These things happen," he said to comfort him. "Women are fickle."

But O'Reilly pressed on with the business of the day. "Now we can do this with violence or without.

It's up to you: The client pays our medical bills, but not yours. Well?"

Once again, reflex politeness took control.

"Ugh—without, please."

And as he sat on the step watching his paltry store of possessions disappear into the back of the truck, Robert realized that his adventures were at an end. This was where the American dream had led him, stranded and impoverished, homeless, worthless, and alone. The truck pulled away. The silence was broken only by the rumble of traffic. He stood up and looked back for the last time at the drab apartment block that once had been the focus of so much hope, but now was just a cold repository of painful memories. Then, without premeditation or deliberation, his legs began to carry him along the scorched deserted sidewalks of the suburbs into the shadow of the towers of wealth, toward the last place on earth he knew that might offer any comfort to a broken man.

The congregation in Al's Bar was at its usual number for the time of day: twenty-five to thirty people watching the hours go by with the relaxed air of those who have nothing better to do and no better place to be. From Al's point of view, it was a good time of day, fresh and clear, when he could talk to his regulars, offer guidance, settle claims, chew the fat. Only last week, for example, he had brokered a settlement between two Italian American families of Sardinian descent, who had sworn vendetta and counter-vendetta against each other for nearly two centuries after a dispute over a mule and a bag of tomatoes. Countless sons had been lost, babies stolen, farm houses torched and writs exchanged, but now, after a few well-chosen words from Al, it was all over. The mule he pointed out, was probably acting of its own accord rather than at the behest of its owner, and perhaps, let's be honest, the tomatoes were less ripe than had subsequently been claimed. And so it was agreed that a no-fault settlement should be applied and the vendettas be de-sworn. That kind of thing was good for business. At least it kept the blood off the seats.

This morning's man with a problem was not so easily consoled. Sitting hunched and morose at the bar, Robert was not an attractive spectacle. He was barely even drinking, just wallowing in melancholy. All attempts by Al to lighten his mood had failed, but with lunchtime approaching, Al did not want Robert there to upset the other customers. A mood like that could be infectious and before he knew it, he would have a dinerful of catatonic depressives, a notoriously poor source of revenue in the catering trade. Okay, so the guy was upset: That waitress, Lily, cute kid, nice legs and so forth, leads the poor schmuck in a dance, and meanwhile she is getting a full workout courtesy of Mr. Muscles. Left Robert standing at the altar, or crying in the chapel, or whatever it was. Well he wasn't the only one. After all, Al was one waitress down now, but you didn't see him sitting at the bar feeling sorry for himself.

"Pull yourself together," Al said.

Robert did not respond.

"She has gone," said Al, "gone to Miami. With

Ryan. The aerobics instructor. They are in love. She ain't never coming back."

Still Robert did not respond.

"Listen, Robert. You're a nice guy. You'll meet someone else. Plenty of fish in the sea. Not for real, obviously, not with all the over-fishing that's going on, no, but figuratively speaking, still plenty of fish. You understand what I am saying: There's a lot of women out there. You're not the first guy who got cheated on, swindled, and dumped. You'll get over it. But not by sitting there upsetting the rest of the customers. You know what you ought to do—you ought to go out there and get a job. When I was a young man—"

"I had a job."

Robert's sudden response took Al by surprise.

"I had a job," said Robert again, to himself rather than Al. "Yesterday I had a job, a girl, an apartment, a life. Everything. And now: nothing. I have nothing. And I ask myself, what went wrong?"

"You got fired," said Al.

Robert looked up slowly and fixed Al with a stare. "Yeah, I got fired. That's when it all started."

For Robert this was a moment of revelation, the moment at which he saw the clear train of events that had led to his downfall, the sequence initiated by one guilty party who had pressed a switch and destroyed his life. Lily? Ryan? What mattered then? Nothing more than unwitting pawns in a larger game.

"This comes right from the top. From Mr. Naville himself." That was what Ms. Gesteten had told him, and from that moment to now he had been in free fall. Now he had come to earth, bruised and

broken at the very bottom, the lowest point of his
life. Clearly he could not stay here. There was no
future at the bottom, no end and no beginning.
There were, he saw with detached clarity, only two
alternatives.

"Al," he said, "the knife." Al reached under the
bar and lifted out the burnished mahogany box.

"What's it going to be?" he asked.

"Revenge," said Robert, "or suicide." The bar
went silent. Drinks did not reach lips, but were
placed carefully down on tables as the customers
turned to look at Robert. Slowly they gathered
around him as he drew his chalk circle. True
enough, he had labeled the halves SUICIDE and RE-
VENGE.

"You're sure?" said Al.

Robert nodded.

Untouched, the lid of the mahogany case sprang
open, startling the crowd. Al looked once more to
Robert, offering retreat, but Robert reached into the
satin-lined box and lifted the knife. Even in the
gloom, its blade sparkled so that it was almost hard
to look at until it had settled on the center of the
circle. There its glow seemed to subside and throb
with contained energy. There was no doubt that it
had sensed the choices on offer, no doubt that it
would decide. Robert gently held the knife at its
pivot, touching the cold metal of the blade and the
rough bestial antler of its handle. It balanced perfectly. He drew one last breath and with the gentlest
flick he set it spinning.

SUICIDE.

The word was simple, its images many. A rope
or a gun, a mouthful of Paraquat or a drop from

a bridge, methods slick and easy and methods botched. Sweet release or the persistent vegetative state.

SUICIDE.

The knife had decided.

"Perhaps you'd better make it the best of three," said Al.

A murmur of assent greeted this. Robert reached forward and spun the knife again.

SUICIDE.

He spun again. And again. And again.

SUICIDE. SUICIDE. SUICIDE. The knife left no room for doubt. Still the crowd urged him on, shouting and cheering, justifying one more spin. But the more often he spun the knife, the clearer it became that suicide was its verdict. Every time it came to rest right in the middle of the suicide half. As he reached his twenty-eighth spin, Robert had given up. He was reconciled to his fate. His life was approaching its end. The crowd, too, sensed that this was a losing battle, but out of sensitivity to the condemned man, they urged one final spin. Robert looked to Al, who nodded.

"Once more," said Robert.

He repeated the simple flick. The knife spun and spun, seeming to revolve forever on its frictionless pivot. But gradually it slowed down and took shape. Now they could watch its final circuits like a bouncing roulette ball. It slowed on REVENGE, but glided on to SUICIDE, then round again to REVENGE. Then just when it seemed it must surely stop at SUICIDE, the knife came to rest on the dividing line. Nobody moved. They hardly breathed for fear of disturbing its equilibrium. They watched and they hoped. Slowly, carefully, Robert slid from his stool and lowered his face to the level of the bar. Closing one eye he checked the position of the blade. The chalk line was thick, not quite straight, and the light was poor but no doubt about it, no doubt at all. At last the knife had decided.

"Revenge!" cried Robert.

A massive cheer rose up and Robert was carried shoulder high to the door, a champion for the common man, the vehicle for all their hopes and fantasies of vengeance upon a cruel world. A vindication for each of their own decisions to keep on going.

Al watched Robert's departure through the door and on to the street. Then Al heard a distinctive high-pitched creaking. He turned to the bar and saw the knife turn slowly through ninety degrees until it came to rest, quite unmistakably, at its chosen destination.

SUICIDE.

7

"**Y**ou shot him through the frontal lobes, so apparently he'll live, but he'll never practice orthodontics again. Do you have any idea how difficult it is to find a good husband in this town? Or a good dentist for that matter?"

Frank Naville was not deficient in anger. Indeed, anger probably held sway as his most abundant characteristic, jostling for prime position with greed, avarice, contempt, brutality, and indignation. All this he knew and he did not care. He knew because after the breakup of his first and only marriage, he had undergone several months of therapy, at the end of which his analyst, clearly shaken by the experience, had declared him a monster devoid of any admirable or even pitiable human characteristics. Naville had been greatly relieved to hear this confirmed: Anger, greed, avarice, and so on had served him well for many years and he would have been distraught to hear of their dilution by compassion or reason or any other of these fashionable modern traits. Anger was his number one; anger was the fuel with which he stoked the fires of his ambition. As a young boy selling cigarettes on the streets of Manhattan, it was anger that had sustained him through heat and cold, poverty and hunger, anger that had driven him on to open a convenience store, then a chain of them, then to sell up and move into power generation, financial speculation, defense contracts, real estate, oil, aviation, and so on. Anger at the world. Anger at anyone who had more than him. There were few industries in which Frank Naville did not now have some interest, and few men who had more than him, but still, as the therapist had identified, still the anger burned.

In recent years, as his wealth accumulated unstoppably around him, he had found time to turn his anger to a subject he had in the past neglected: his daughter. Celine, as the only issue from the eight-year marriage, was a focus of confused emotion for Naville. On the one hand, she was, of course, his daughter and he loved her beyond all things; but on the other hand, she was also his ex-wife's daughter and therefore a reminder of that singularly unhappy time. Furthermore, while he wished her an easy and happy life, unlike his own, to see her idling her days away easy and happy, had driven him mad with anger.

And then there was the subject of men. As his little girl became a beautiful woman, he was all too aware of the sharks gathering and had done his best to deter them with a display of rudeness that discouraged all but the most insensitive. His dismay at her choice of male companions was allayed only slightly by their short-lived presence in her life. Not one seemed to have any real worth, any balls—at least not until this Elliot fellow. He was a man of experience, a man of independent means, and though he made little effort to disguise his designs on Celine's inheritance, at least he was honest in this respect. And if he had upset Celine from time to time, well, perhaps that was what she needed. Besides, he was the city's most sought-after and expensive dentist—or had been until the recent "accident" by the swimming pool.

Only immediate intervention by Naville and the heavy use of bribery and threats had prevented a major front-page scandal. The D.A. had also been very obliging, taking the view that the injury was essentially self-inflicted, in return for a cash donation of $150,000 transferred in a parking lot with no ceremony.

But all this had brought Naville's anger to the boil, and convinced him that the time had come for him to sort out his daughter's life since clearly she would not do it for herself. And so Celine found herself in her father's office, unaware of his agenda as once again he found fault with her behavior.

"Playing these games," he continued, "you have disgraced yourself once more. My fear is that without guidance and purpose, you'll end up like your mother, who long ago found her own natural level in society. That is to say she scuttles along the bottom."

Celine once more inspected her perfect fingernails and wondered if her life was not simply a long and tedious dream from which she would soon awaken to find that never again would she hear a lecture from this man who was her father. Today's lecture had been longer and, even by her father's absurd standards, angrier than usual. Celine was aware that somehow she distressed her father, but felt powerless and disinclined to do anything about it, since she was due at any moment to wake up and leave all this behind.

"Her biggest problem," she said in response to his comments about his ex-wife, "was marrying a man like you: a mistake I have taken great care to avoid." There, she felt, that should do it. That kind of direct abuse usually sent him over the edge, bringing the lecture to a heart-stopping, expletive-laden termination.

But today Naville suppressed his rage, or at least he contained the excess, for today he had something else to say, another surprise to deliver. He concentrated on breathing and gazed from the window to steady himself. Far below him a young man almost caused an accident as he darted through the traffic at an intersection, but this was of no interest to Naville.

He turned back to his daughter. God strike him dead if she wasn't the living image of her mother. Naville recalled the night they met, in a New York dance hall, 1969. With money in his pocket, the young Francis Naville was a weekend hippie and had a date with some "chick" whose name he did not recall but whose clumsy feet and heavy black workshoes he would never forget. As she trod all over his sandals during the opening bars of "San Francisco (Be Sure to Wear Some Flowers in Your Hair)" his eyes met those of another woman. Her partner seemed every bit as inept as his own. They

had smiled at their shared misfortune and somehow finished the dance in each other's arms. Romance had blossomed, marriage followed, and then
they seemed to go their separate ways in a haze of
accusation and recrimination over who drove
whom to what with their unacceptable behavior.
And then it was all over, with nothing to show but
a few scratch marks, a brutal divorce settlement,
and a hundred-and-ten-pound living, walking,
breathing memento called Celine.

"You're going to go to work," he told her.

Robert had not been killed at the intersection, but
it had been a near thing. The knife would have ap-
proved, but Robert felt a stronger call. His sprint
across the road had taken him to the steps of his
former workplace, the scene of his unfair and catastrophic dismissal, where he would track down and
confront his sworn enemy, the man at the top: Francis Naville, Mr. Corporate Fat himself.

Attempting to blend with the other employees,
Robert climbed the broad stone steps and followed
a small herd of suited junior executives through the
smoked-glass portal and into the lobby. From there
they moved toward the reception desk where all
staff, no matter how familiar, were supposed to
show their identity cards to a man called Zbryskis.

Robert had walked past Zbryskis countless
times, but exchanged no words. Of each other's
lives each knew nothing, but without a valid pass,
Robert understood that Zbryskis should in theory
stop him from going farther. Robert believed that in
practice however, reception security was a tedious

and unrewarding task, that unless an intruder looked like a Martian or the leader of the Hell's Angels local chapter, Zbryskis was unlikely to rouse himself from open-eyed slumber.

The junior executives surged past, giving him nothing more than a cursory glimpse of their cards. Zbryskis did not move, gazing straight ahead like a goldfish who has discovered chewing gum and seeks no higher pleasure in life. Robert followed, fumbling in his pocket as though he, too, were about to produce a card. Zbryskis continued to stare straight ahead. As Robert had correctly forecast, he was looking principally for members of an alien species or a representative of Hell's Angels, but there was one further category which would show up on his radar, one which Robert had not included: smart-ass, wannabe novelist, illegal immigrant, recently dismissed, vengeful ex-janitors.

Zbryskis went to condition red. His eyes swiveled toward Robert and engaged with his cortex, banishing a sweet fantasy about running naked with slave girls through olive groves in ancient Rome, and confirming the presence of a Category Three intruder. Further frantic activity in his brain produced an audible level-one vocal response.

"Stop."

And everyone stopped. It had been so long since anyone had heard Zbryskis speak, that the effect of his command was lobby paralysis. If he had shouted, "Go," the effect would have been the same. Even Robert, with more motive than most to keep on going, was momentarily arrested by shock. Zbryskis, it was clear, could speak. There was no telling where this might end. If he now chose to demand his pass and bar his entry, there would be nothing Robert could do. His plan for revenge would fall at the first hurdle.

The tension was unbearable. Twenty pairs of eyes focused on Zbryskis. Slowly he licked his lips. His Adam's apple rose and fell and he inhaled deeply. In his red-alerted mind he assembled one by one the components of a phrase that would expose this intruder, but so many years had elapsed since last he had spoken that words did not come easily.

A clock ticked loudly in the lobby.

Zbryskis was aware of the expectation. He opened his mouth.

"Show me your pass," was what he intended to say.

"Go now, to the olive groves of Livinia," was what came out.

The spell was broken. People moved. Zbryskis, relieved to have spoken, resumed his silence. Robert, equally relieved, needed no further encouragement and he followed the suited executives into the waiting elevator. As the door closed and he pressed the button for the top floor, he wondered who Livinia was and whether they would ever meet. He regretted all the times he had walked past Zbryskis with no inkling of the complex depths that lay behind his deep under-sea gaze. Momentarily he wanted to get out, to tell Zbryskis this, to apologize, to take him out for a drink, swap stories, go bowling, sleep on his couch, raid his refrigerator, borrow his car, become a buddy, a human friend in a cold world. But it was too late. The doors closed and the moment was gone.

* * *

Celine was still recovering from the shock of her father's announcement. Panic gripped her mind and a sick miserable feeling lay in her stomach.

Go to work.

The very words were ugly enough, but the prospect in reality was almost unbearable. Celine was no fool: She knew that someone had to work, that work could be rewarding, interesting, sociable, and profitable. Of all that there was no doubt. She did not challenge anyone else's right to work. She would even encourage it. Since there was obviously so much work to be done in the world, and the more that was done by everybody else, the less was the chance that there would be any left for her. And yet work was the prospect that now stared her in the face. "Nine to five." She had heard the expression and she did not care for it, nor for its even more distasteful variants—eight 'til six, eight 'til eight, and so on; nor for its unspoken implications— breakfast meetings, working evenings at home, responsibility, schedules, the list of horrors was endless.

And it wasn't as if she didn't work already. She spent her father's money, or at least some fraction of it. She remained fit and beautiful, for what that was worth. She broke hearts and shot dentists. And if all that didn't amount to work, then what was it? If it was supposed to be fun, then that was news to her, because none of it had made her outstandingly happy for longer than a few seconds at a time. It felt like work. Surely it was work. But now her father was going on and on about his vision of work and how it related to her. His tirade was continuous, a dam burst of anger sweeping away all protest and carrying her helpless toward the polluted cold ocean of work.

"You have spent a quarter of a century watching the sun rise behind one clump of palm trees and set behind another," he told her, "but tomorrow, you will work. This is it, the new dawn. You will work here, under my direct supervision, every day, for a salary. You will learn the essence of business: How to generate a profit from a loss and a loss from a profit. You will learn about money and how it flows back relentlessly toward he who owns it. You will work."

And on he went.

The elevator had gradually parted company with its passengers, altitude of disembarkation correlating directly with expense and understatement of suit, until only one man remained inside. Defying the trend, he was heading toward the top floor in a worn casual jacket, jeans, and tennis shoes. The smell of whiskey on his breath competed with the odor of sweat that surrounded him. He was unshaven, irritable, and hyperventilating. Fear and fury radiated from his twitching limbs. He did not know what he was going to do, but undoubtedly, he would do it.

When the elevator came to rest and the door opened at the end of its journey, Robert stepped out and saw immediately the channel for his revenge. Twenty yards away along the corridor a small robot was hard at work. Ignorant of the misery it had generated, the robot swept and polished as if made for the task, which of course it was. About two feet high and the same in diameter, its squat torso was supported on four rubber wheels. A vacuum extended like a trunk sweeping back and forth, and two spindly articulated limbs polished and buffed the vinyl flooring. As it progressed slowly toward Robert, it emitted a regular, pulsating low-pitched *bleep*.

He picked it up carefully, expecting it to squeal or struggle like a fractious cat, but it did not waver from its task. The perfect automaton, it continued to suck, buff, and polish the thin air where the floor should have been. Robert supported its weight with his right hand as he tucked the machine under his left arm and strode with renewed purpose toward the office door marked with unfussy silver lettering: FRANCIS NAVILLE.

Inside the office Naville was still in search of new methods of torment to reveal to his shell-shocked daughter.

"Yes, you will work," he repeated for the umpteenth time, savoring again the uncluttered simplicity and the deep resonance of the phrase. "Now, that may not strike you as very palatable. It may make you want to vomit. You will however get used to the taste and pretty soon you will be spooning it down and asking for more like all the other kids." At which point the door of his office was kicked open by a young man holding a robot.

* * *

Zbryskis had not been entirely unaffected by the events in the lobby. He knew that he had failed to deal with the intruder situation as he should have done and sensed that on some intangible level his failure was linked with the Fall of Rome, but he could not understand the ineffectiveness of the phrase, "Show me your pass," since this was quite clearly what he had said. Mulling this over and seeking to amend his personal failings, he had arrived at the following conclusion: The intruder's desperation and reluctance to show his pass indicated beyond doubt that he was a violent and dangerous man. Zbryskis reached under his desk and pressed a large red button. In years to come they would say, "This was his finest hour," for with that small gesture he had given the signal: General Security Alert.

Robert stepped into the office and addressed his enemy. "Mr. Naville, I presume."

Naville, taken by surprise, said nothing. Celine sitting back near the wall sighed with relief. She thought the old man would never shut up, but thankfully this interruption promised some diversion.

Robert had not noticed Celine. He was focused only on Naville, from whom he needed no confirmatory identification. This was his man.

"Now you may think you can replace me with a robot. Well, get this."

Gathering his strength, he propped the robot up on his right hand as if he were about to put a giant shot. With a grunt, he launched it.

Oh, thought Celine, an industrial dispute. She had read of such matters. Another good reason, she felt, not to go to work. How appropriate that it should unfold in front of her on this day. She watched the robot describe an arc through the air as it sailed toward the giant plate-glass window, through which it would surely pass unhindered to fall seventy stories to the street below, delivering who knew what carnage and random unhappiness to those in its path.

Robert felt a twinge of guilt at this prospect.

Naville felt no twinge of anything, partly because carnage and unhappiness did not offend him, but mainly because he knew, as Robert did not, that for reasons of personal security he was surrounded in his office by windows of reinforced security glass. If a bullet could not penetrate, then a robot, he knew, would not even register a crack.

It bounced as Naville expected off the transparent barrier and landed wheels to the floor. Unaffected by its experience, it immediately began sucking, buffing, and polishing as though nothing had happened.

Robert's dismay was Naville's joy. A more unequivocal demonstration of the machine's superiority over its flesh-and-blood counterpart would have been hard to devise. Naville resolved to dismiss the entire department: This was the future.

Robert's protest was fizzling out; his anticlimactic nondestruction of his metal foe had left him disarmed and weary. All that remained open to him was to deliver an insulting good-bye and then depart with dignity. But just as he prepared the insult, he was submerged beneath a mountain of beefy blue-clad flesh.

The security unit at Naville Holdings did not get much excitement, and never in more than ten years' existence had they experienced the thrill of General Security Alert. They had trained, certainly, but mainly by eating doughnuts, so that on arrival in their employer's office, having shifted their many hundreds of collective pounds of flab at unaccustomed speed along uncomfortable long corridors, it was as much as most of them could do simply to launch themselves on the first human they came to which, fortunately for them, was Robert.

Although winded by the impact, Robert quickly realized that he was under attack. Punches and kicks, none delivered with great expertise but painful enough all the same, were raining down on his back, arms, and legs. He lashed out with his elbows and fists, catching his assailants sometimes on bone or joint, but more often in vast acres of unnamed flesh. It was as though he was fighting a marshmallow grizzly bear.

Celine watched the spectacle with interest. As a contest it was obviously deficient, but as education there was much to commend. This she thought was what "work" was probably like on a regular basis. There you were, in your penthouse office, trying to fritter away the day with some sort of executive toy or catching some sleep perhaps, when inevitably a group of irate men would start fighting in front of you. Day after day. Nine to five. At least. The prospect was appalling.

Her father did not watch the spectacle at all. He had turned to face the window and was rehearsing the second installment of the speech he would make to Celine. It was to be calm but suffused with underlying anger, a clinical recital of her mother's many faults and failings, or at least the top one hundred, each referenced to a specific example, place and date provided, adding up to an all-round damning, unanswerable, watertight condemnation of the woman. The sighs, groans, and thumps behind him were only a distraction. Naville was not interested enough to look.

If he had been, he would have noticed the large dark patches of sweat forming under the armpits of his crack security unit, and their heavy breathing as they tired of the effort of clenching their podgy fingers into fists and raising them up to pummel the wiry resilient form beneath them. One or two, he would have seen, were pulling their punches and even seemed to be dreaming of doughnuts. He missed also Robert's face, nearly blue as he lay crushed at the base of the heap, gasping for breath and his arms flailing helplessly. It was in mid-flail that his right had connected with something hard, metallic, and smooth. His fingers eased around it and he held on tightly, hoping to use it as a lever to pull himself up. But as soon as he began to pull, the lever came away in his hand and Robert found, to his surprise, that he was holding a gun.

In the speech Naville was composing in his mind, he had reached item number twenty-eight: untidiness. Date, May 4, 1974. Place, home. Leaves pair of shoes at bottom of stairs.

"Everybody stand still!" shouted Robert.

Suddenly the security unit, with a level of coor-

dination and effort absent from their performance
so far, sprang up and away.

Celine sat up, even more interested. Perhaps she
had been a little harsh on "work."

Naville turned in time to see Robert stand up
and wheel around with the gun, startling the security unit into a nervous circle.

A smile crept onto Robert's lips as he considered
the possibility that he may have gained an advantage.

To Celine's detached and more critical eye, however, it appeared that a circle was not the optimum
formation in which to keep his enemy, as it left him
exposed at any time to a surprise assault. Furthermore, his constant rotating to keep everyone "covered" soon made him giddy so that when Loafer, a
large man with a mustache, a fifty-four-inch waist
and a reputation within the unit for mental agility
and physical fitness, swung a haymaker, there was
little Robert could do but take it and fall.

Which he did.

The gun slipped from his grasp and slid along
the floor toward Celine. The blue mound descended
again, pummeling with renewed vigor, partly out
of frustration, and partly because this time Naville
was watching. They punched, kicked, kneed, el-
bowed, and crushed Robert. If there had been any
hint of professionalism about them, he would have
been dead. But it still looked like plenty of beating.
Naville watched now with approval. Young upstart.
This would teach him, teach anyone. He would let
it go on until there was a decent bit of blood on the
floor. Naville had used real hard men in the past to

break disputes in sweatshops and was not averse to violence as a problem solver.

Celine did not watch with approval. Watching people being beaten up was, like so much in life, not the fun it first promised to be. The inequality of the contest was beginning to discomfort her, all the more so as her father was clearly enjoying every moment of it. She looked at him, smug malice on his face as he watched the assault, the same expression as in his own assault, albeit of a different kind, on her way of life. Closer to Celine, down on the floor, the victim of all this was barely visible beneath the blue, sweating mass. All that she could see was one arm, outstretched as though begging for mercy or relief. Closer still to her feet lay the gun, symbol of his moment of resistance.

No one noticed it.

It was an act of unconscious will.

She kicked the gun back along the floor toward the man's outstretched arm, to the hand that begged for mercy or relief.

Underneath the mountain, the breath being squeezed from his lungs and sense being punched from his brain, seeing nothing but darkness, Robert felt the gun make contact with his hand. Second time around, the contour was familiar and he did not hesitate. The sound of the gun firing took them all by surprise, deafeningly loud in the office despite its presidential dimensions. Plaster trickled down from the ceiling where the bullet had lodged.

Once again the security unit leaped back as one, but this time Robert, energized by experience and an anger of his own, did not allow them to form their circle.

"Hit the floor! Everyone down on the floor!" he ordered, waving the gun carelessly.

The security unit dropped to the floor.

Celine nodded in approval. Tactically, the young man appeared to be a fast learner, but commands to hit the floor were not, she felt, designed to include her. In that respect, they were like social niceties—educational goals, organized religion, line dancing, or the conventions of drug taking, healthy eating, and fashion. So she remained in her seat.

Her father also declined to hit the floor. But if the girl had barely registered on Robert's consciousness, the same was not true of Naville.

"Down on the floor," Robert repeated, this time pointing the gun directly at Naville. With as much dignity as was possible and what he considered was an air of defiance, Naville lowered himself to the floor.

Robert collected his thoughts. As far as he could tell, he held the advantage now. All his physical opponents were cowering on the floor and even his sworn enemy, Naville himself, was at his mercy. He realized that his situation was ridiculous, unsustainable. He had never intended that revenge should go this far, that he should end up holding a gun to a man's head. It all just seemed to have escalated beyond his control. But what of it? There was no going back now.

"I want my job back."

Naville said nothing. He too recognized the unsustainable nature of Robert's situation. He could see that the young man had waded well beyond his depth and lacked the will to swim. If their positions were reversed, Naville would have had no compunction about pumping a couple of shots into Robert. With every second that passed as Robert failed to do just that, Naville felt the balance of power tilt in his direction.

Robert knew his bluff was being called. He had to do something and do it soon, before Loafer got that heroic feeling again.

A tense silence filled the room, disturbed only by the sound of Robert's rapid breathing and a regular, pulsating, low-pitched *bleep*. As he registered the source of the *bleep*, Robert swiveled toward the security unit, which let out a flutter of panic. But he fired over them, three shots. The first and second lodged in the wall, but the third found its target. The robot faltered, mortally wounded, but determined to clean on. Its vacuum trunk jerked spasmodically back and forth, and its spindly little limbs spun in the air. The *bleeps* became louder and more frequent until the robot was emitting a harsh continuous tone.

Robert fired again.

A series of internal explosions rocked the machine. It staggered back across the floor like a wounded cowboy before toppling over and coming to rest. The tone spluttered and stopped. The vacuum lay limp and motionless. One of the rubber wheels spun slowly, and then it was all over. Encouraged by his own display of firepower, Robert turned back to his ex-employer.

"Okay, I want what I had before, Mr. Naville."

But Naville was not impressed. Anyone, he reasoned, could shoot a robot, but to shoot a man took guts. He felt no danger. Nothing more was going to happen. Let the young jerk have his moment. It wouldn't last.

"I'm going to count to five, Mr. Naville, and if you don't promise me my job back—I'm going to kill you."

There. He had done it: named his price and identified the penalty.

But still Naville was not scared. If anything, he was pleased—at least this was progress. A count to five, no price paid, no penalty extracted, the young fool disarmed and arrested, then back to work for one and all.

Robert began counting.

"One."

Naville said nothing.

"Two."

Nothing.

"Three."

This was getting near the bit that Robert was dreading. Stark choices beckoned. He held the gun trained on Naville.

"Four."

Naville remained silent. The men of the security unit placed their fingers in their ears and squinted toward the scene a few feet away. But nothing happened. Robert was frozen at four. The men eased the fingers from their ears. He wasn't going to do it.

He couldn't.

He knew it. They knew it. Naville knew it. Four was his limit.

"Five," said Celine.

And he did it.

Not in the head, fortunately, for with the shock of hearing a woman's voice, Robert had swung around and the bullet had lodged in Naville's thigh, and already a large crimson puddle was spreading across the floor. Naville screamed and clutched at his leg, messages of pain and destruction flooding his brain. Robert looked down at his victim, horrified.

"Oh my God," he said, moving to step back, but Naville grasped his ankle and Robert's attempts to shake him off succeeded only in spreading the puddle still farther.

Robert turned to look at the woman. She was smiling.

This was the best show Celine had ever watched. There had been a weird bit where the guy with the gun had demanded his job back (like, why?) but after that the standoff, the threats, the shooting (two out of ten for accuracy) had been worth every minute of her time. And now her father was actually wounded. That looked like a lot of blood. More than with Elliot. Of course, any amount of blood always looked like a lot. Even so, this looked like it might actually be fatal or at least pretty near it. She went to have a closer look. Her father was predictably furious in the midst of his suffering, but surprisingly the guy with the gun didn't seem too happy either.

"What did you say that for?" he bellowed.

"Five comes directly after four," replied Celine.

"I know that," said Robert.

Who was this woman? What was she doing? Why had she interfered?

"I thought maybe you had a problem," said Celine, "with numeracy. It's nothing to be ashamed of—I mean without access to a good education."

"Shut up!"

"Only trying to help."

"I don't need any help."

He tried again to shake Naville from his ankle, but he clung tightly and would not be removed.

"You'll die for this," said Naville. "I swear you'll die for this."

Robert was beginning to panic. He was aware of the girl talking again.

"You could shoot him again if you like," she said. "Maybe through the head this time. I'll count to five and—"

"Shut up," said Robert.

"Who are you anyway?" he asked her, but it was Naville who replied first.

"She's nobody."

Celine smiled again and looked deep and directly into Robert's eyes.

"Don't you know? I'm his daughter."

8

"**D**rive!" shouted Robert for the second time, waving the gun in the air. But Celine did not. Obeying commands was not, as we know, her strong suit. Besides, she was not inclined to cooperate with a plan that deviated from her own. In announcing her identity to the unemployed gunman, she had expected to generate respect, not abduction. Certainly, she had foreseen a joint departure from the office, but not like this. The journey down in the elevator from penthouse to parking lot had taken place without any of the conspiratorial clubbiness that she had hoped for. Far from it: Relations between them had been frosty and antagonistic throughout. He had insisted on pointing the gun at her head, and although she did not fear him, she had more than enough sense to be frightened of the gun. Her demand that he direct it elsewhere had been ignored and several times she expected to die when the elevator stopped and the doors opened to reveal a crowd of screaming employees. At such times his anxiety was clearly off the scale and death nothing more than a squeeze away.

On reaching the parking level, he had shoved her without ceremony toward and then into her father's black Lincoln Town Car, for which he had taken the keys before leaving the office.

And now he expected her to drive. It was all just too much. The thrill of combat was over and Celine wanted to go home.

Robert would also have been happy to go home, except that home was several thousand miles away, and from where he sat the only way that he could see himself getting there was via deportation at the end of a lengthy sentence in his local neighborhood correctional facility. When she said she was Naville's daughter, it was like a ray of light that shone the way, a sign from above even: Kidnap the daughter. It had seemed so right that no second thought was given. It was the key to everything: revenge, escape, leverage all rolled into one. But no sooner had he initiated their escape via the elevator, then the second thoughts began to undermine him. All those people were screaming at *him*, he realized. It was spooky. Made him feel like a monster. And then this girl: something wasn't right, something was far from right. What was she? The poisoned chalice that would finish him off? Damn woman wouldn't even start the car.

"Will you just drive?" he shouted again, enunciating every syllable as in the rearview mirror he saw the security unit beginning to re-form near the exit ramp. Drawing their guns this time, he noticed.

"I can't," Celine shouted back.

"What?" said Robert.

"I don't know how," she replied.

Just his luck, Robert thought, and how appropriate to the downward spiral of his life: He had installed in the driving seat the only able-bodied adult in the entire Union who could not drive. It was utterly improbable, but as his life was going, it was that utter improbability that made it so inevitable. But still he could hardly believe it.

"You can't drive?"

"No."

"Well, why not?"

"I never learned."

"But why?" he demanded with real curiosity. "Why did you never learn?"

"I didn't need to," she replied.

Of course, he realized. She didn't need to. The guards were closing in, moving from pillar to pillar. She didn't need to. Why should she? Rich girl, Naville's daughter, probably got driven everywhere. Or flown more likely. Or didn't need to go anywhere, because everywhere came to her. So simple, so reasonable, nothing sinister. She never learned because she didn't need to.

"Well, now you do," he told her as he turned the ignition and the engine sparked into life. "Press that pedal to go faster, that one to go slower, that lever forward to go forward and back to go back. The rest you can pick up as you go along."

The guards were lined up between them and the exit ramp.

"Now drive," he said, more calmly, adding this time, "please."

And Celine put her foot to the floor.

* * *

And the rest she did pick up as she went along. Indeed, given the fuss that everyone made about learning to drive, Celine felt it was surprisingly easy. All you had to do was drive in as straight a line as possible and not distract yourself worrying about other cars. Corners were a problem, especially at speed, as were intersections unless you kept that foot down hard. All in all, Celine felt she had proven herself something of a natural in this endeavor, and as they cruised through the third red light—stopping was discretionary for the natural—she attempted some light conversation to relax the passenger.

"What's your name?"

"Robert," he told her.

He still held the gun. He was drenched in sweat, shivering in the air-conditioned microclimate.

"I'm Celine," she told him.

He winced as a truck crossed their path and Celine failed to brake. All this to die in a crash.

"Where are we going?" asked Celine.

"Never mind," snapped Robert, "drive more carefully."

"He cut in on me," said Celine, an even faster learner at the defensive, self-justifying tone of the reckless driver.

"Mirror. Signal. Maneuver," Robert said, invoking the sacred mantra of his own driving lessons in a time and a land faraway.

"Mirror, signal, maneuver."

And that was it, conversation-wise, for several minutes. A painful awkwardness followed this exchange. Celine began to drive a little more carefully. She stopped at two lights in succession. She even looked in the mirror, but found nothing of any interest.

Robert was thinking. He did not know where to begin. The whole sequence of cause and effect had expanded beyond his understanding and here he was in a stolen car with a kidnapped woman and a gun. He felt he should say something, but what? Something reassuring? What message would that send? Weakness, lack of purpose? Or how about something threatening? He tried to work out whether it would be easier to escalate or to pull back on the reassurance–threat scale if he found he had said the wrong thing. He gave up. What about something practical? He could think of nothing practical. Maybe he should ask an innocuous question. His turn to break the ice. But all he could think of were the pointless questions with which, as a gauche adolescent, he had attempted to strike up relationships with awesomely mature girls.

—What's your favorite record shop?

—Don't have one.

End of conversation.

Robert drummed his fingers and attempted to appear busy, deep in constructive thought, but constructive thought was impossible. He couldn't go on like this. No matter what was at stake, if this carried on, he would be letting her out at a bus station within the hour, the kidnapping equivalent of asking for the check, splitting it, and resolving to meet again sometime. And why not? After all this was a kidnapping: If it ended with anything less than his incarceration he would consider himself fortunate.

Robert had been brought up according to two relevant maxims which were now directly in opposition with one another. They were: A. Never talk to strangers, and B. Speak politely to women. Trawling through his store of etiquette he could find no resolution to this conflict, no mention of kidnapping. In truth, he was deeply uncomfortable with the whole situation.

"You're not very comfortable with this situation, are you?" said Celine.

"I'm fine," replied Robert immediately. "What on earth makes you think I'm not comfortable?"

"You're not saying anything. You're trying hard to think of something to say, but you can't, and the more you think about it, the worse it gets, if you see what I mean. It's like when you're young and you're hanging out, there is always some guy who can't think of anything normal to say so he always ends up asking you some dumb pointless question like what's your favorite—"

"I'm not thinking about it!"

"What?"

"Whatever you're talking about. Nothing, I mean I am thinking about what we are going to do now."

"Good." She left a questioning silence which Robert could not deflect.

"Well?" she asked when he failed to respond.

"Well, what?"

"Do you know what you're doing?"

"I know exactly what I'm doing." He had no idea. "We are going to drive for a while. Then . . . then we'll go somewhere."

Even as he said it, he felt it was pretty good. A

little thin maybe, still a little detail to fill in and flesh out, but a solid base of a plan, no question of it.

"That's it?" said Celine.

"So far."

"You're a real evil genius."

"Standard kidnap protocol."

A less awkward silence descended. Robert felt better now, having defined his plan, albeit rather sketchily. The kidnapping had thus been green lighted in his mind and there was no need for small talk. Celine drove for three hours, through the thinning suburbs with their lawns and families, into the agricultural belt and then out beyond the irrigation and into the scrubland where the road lay straight and long toward the hills now visible in the distance. They had not been pursued and Celine did not expect that they would be. She knew her father's modus operandi.

As the sun cast long shadows in the late afternoon, she steered the car toward a lonely gas station where a young man named Walt awaited their arrival with open-hearted and uninhibited enthusiasm.

Walt was the perfect employee. Ostensibly the lowest form of life in a vast chain of gas stations, Walt's enthusiasm for the corporate vision was a match for anyone's. The providing of gas was to Walt not merely a mechanical act but the holistic endorsement of an entire way of life. "Refueling" he had realized was an act of great symbolic importance, especially out here in the middle of nowhere, representing an opportunity to take stock of life's achievements and plan for the future. Walt liked to challenge outdated divisions between driver and passenger, and engage in free and open discussion, and provide an opportunity to refuel the spirit for the journey ahead. It was all so beautiful, so perfect, so true, that sometimes he would weep at the end of a shift.

It was in this spirit of evangelism that he prepared to greet the young couple who pulled in with the black Lincoln. One look at them and he knew: They were in desperate need of refueling. Their journey was not long begun and they had far to go, but look, they were tired, irritable, not speaking, clearly uncomfortable with each other. What sorry train of events, he wondered, had brought them to such an unhappy pass? A dispute about map reading? Financial concerns? Infidelity? Walt would never know. His business was not to know but only to heal.

"Afternoon, ma'am," he began as the window was lowered, "afternoon, sir, my name is Walt and I'm here to help you in any way that I can during your visit to us, be it short or long, and whether it is purely for refueling purposes or for the use of our extensive washroom and retail facilities. So let me start by asking you: What may I do for you today?"

"Is this a gas station, Walt?" Robert asked.

"Sure is, sir."

"Then fill the tank with gas and cut the crap," Robert said as he plucked the keys from the ignition and threw them toward Walt, who fumbled and let them fall.

Celine sighed as Walt picked up the keys from the ground. She had felt like this so many times before, at expensive restaurants with brash young men who sought to impress her by bullying those less powerful than themselves. Men like Elliot sending back the wine because it was from the wrong side of the valley.

"The guy is just doing his job," she said, "just trying to be helpful."

Robert was silent. He knew she was right: Walt was just trying to be helpful, and he had overreacted. But that wasn't his fault. All he wanted was gas. Why did the guy have to spout out all that consumer-friendly vision speak? Couldn't he see that Robert was under stress?

Celine compounded his misery.

"You know something," she said, "you're in deep trouble. My father is going to have you killed."

This was true.

"You realize that?" she asked.

Robert said nothing. Behind them they could hear the pump and the flow of gas.

"Tortured first, naturally," she added in the interest of accuracy, "then killed."

Tortured and killed. Not just tortured, which implied some sort of life afterward, and not just killed, which implied something swift, but both.

"What if I let you go?" asked Robert.

"What do you expect? That he is going to forgive you? You kidnap his daughter and shoot him in the leg and he is going to forgive you?"

"Hold on there. Forgive?" Robert said, inspired and reanimated. "Why should I ask him for forgiveness? Let's remember what happened: He treated me like shit, like I was nobody, just because I was a cleaner. Like I was disposable."

Robert paused, his index finger frozen in midair,

jabbing toward Celine, who shrank back in her seat. From behind, a cough interrupted the moment.

"That's the tankful, sir," Walt said.

"Thank you, Walt," Celine said taking the keys.

Robert reached into his jacket and pulled out a handful of bills. "How much is that?"

"Thirty dollars, sir."

From what he had heard, Walt understood that the unhappiness of this couple was connected to a problem with family relationships. This was common. There was a time when Walt would have considered such unhappiness insoluble, judging by the man's behavior on arrival. But experience had given Walt faith in the power of refueling and now he believed that all wounds could be healed.

Robert peeled off three ten-dollar bills and handed them to Walt.

"Thank you, sir," said Walt.

Robert peeled off five ones and held them out toward him. Walt hesitated, unsure of the significance. This was not expected. Rejuvenation of the soul, certainly, a reaffirmation of love, possibly, but normally confined within the cabin of the car, not expressed outwardly, for Walt did not seek personal gain. He was merely the agent of refueling. Service was its own reward.

"Take it," said Robert. A lump was forming in Robert's throat. He struggled to find the words to express the solidarity and kinship he felt with this man to whom he had been so thoughtlessly rude. Walt hesitated.

"Go on, Walt. For you."

Walt reached in slowly and took the worn bills

from Robert's grip. He folded them into his back pocket.

"You're a man," said Robert, as much to himself as Walt, "not a slave, not a machine and don't let anyone ever treat you otherwise."

He turned to Celine with calm purpose.

"Drive."

As Walt watched them depart, vanishing into the vastness of the continent, he knew that he had been changed. All these years, he had been mistaken. He had been aiming too low. Underselling himself. But now his goal was clear. Sure, he was doing good work here at the gas station, but it wasn't just folks who passed through who needed him, it wasn't just them he could help. There was a whole nation of men and women out there, treated like slaves, like machines, denied the pursuit of life and liberty that was every citizen's right. He could bring healing, he could bring freedom, he could bring love, not just to one man or one woman, but to all men, to all women. Heck, it wasn't just the occasional passerby who needed refueling, it was America. America needed refueling. How far had they traveled, how long the journey, how weary was the spirit? Why, you could see it all around you—in the poverty, in the inner cities, in the racial strife, in the disillusionment with big government, in the growing gulf between those who had and those who did not. America, Walt realized, was dying of thirst: America was crying out so loud and clear, crying out day and night, for refueling.

All this Walt saw in an instant, a blazing vision of his own destiny. He saw it clear and true and he knew that one day he, Walt, would be President of the United States of America.

9

Darkness had long since fallen on the isolated landscape. In the dense forests of pine that coated the hills, furry creatures large and small went about their nocturnal business of killing and eating each other. In the lonely dark cabin nothing stirred. In the black Lincoln, a man and a woman sat and watched. Four thousand feet above sea level, with the sky clear and sparkling, the air was cold and their breath condensed on the windshield. Their clothing, so appropriate to the hot city day, was perceptibly inadequate for their new environment, even while they sat in the insulated confines of the car.

Robert resisted the falling temperature while he watched the cabin for signs of life. Celine, however, was neither watching nor resisting. She was just cold.

"It's empty," she said. This evoked no response. "I'm cold."

Again, Robert ignored her.

"I want to go inside," she added.

"Well," said Robert, "we're not going inside yet."

"I think it's empty," said Celine.

"I don't care what you think."

Robert did not want to discuss this. He just wanted to be sure it was empty because he did not like what was coming next. But she wouldn't shut up.

"I have the right to my opinion."

Robert couldn't let this pass. He flicked on the overhead light and turned toward her.

"No, no, no," he said, "in this situation, you have no rights, so I don't need to care what you think and we stay here until I'm ready to move. Do you understand?"

He waited for her reply. Instead, she flicked the light off and looked away.

"I'm cold," she said in a simple, matter-of-fact tone that said "I will not dignify your cruelty with discussion nor plead beyond the facts of my case."

Robert seethed silently. This was typical of a woman arguing with you without arguing. He felt like an inquisitor trying to torch a heretic who keeps saying, "I believe in God," in an irritating, self-righteous way. Robert considered offering Celine this comparison, but there was no point. It would only have ended up with him becoming more and more tangled up in the web of his own self-justification, sounding less and less convincing while she softly intoned, "I'm cold," all rosy cheeked and glowing with the virginal purity of her simple argument.

"I'm cold," she said.

"Right," said Robert, getting out of the car and slammed the door shut.

Outside it was even colder, but at least, Robert felt, the air was fresh and clean. The cabin was not far away, perhaps forty yards, and there certainly did not seem to be anyone around. After the long journey and all that waiting, it was a relief to be outside, to stretch his legs and get away from that woman and her incessant complaints. Robert, whistling softly, set off along the remainder of the rough track that led to the cabin.

Celine watched him go and sighed. Arguing without arguing was not her style at all. She hated that kind of prissy, holier-than-thou behavior, but under the circumstances she felt it was the only way forward. Normal arguing and the issuing of direct commands had failed. She did not wish to sit in the car all night, and "I'm cold" had worked. Ends justified means.

Routinely she checked the ignition, but he had taken the keys. It was only to be expected. This had not been a good day so far and the only positive aspect of it all was that one act of misfortune (being kidnapped) had sort of temporarily cancelled out another (going to work). So long as she was held against her will in a remote mountain cabin at the whim of a disgruntled, sacked employee, her father could hardly expect her to turn up for work. That was certainly the silver lining, though the texture of the cloud remained uncertain.

* * *

Robert meanwhile had stopped whistling after about ten yards, and after twenty, he had stopped walking. It was the noises that stopped him. All those blades of grass swishing against each other, boughs creaking and wind buffeting resonant mountain walls. And then there were the sounds of the animals: scraping, crunching, and flapping. He looked toward the cabin. Simultaneously it had grown larger and darker and had moved farther away. He was now approaching a palace of gothic terror across a mile of poisonous, wolf-infested terrain. He looked back at the car. Simultaneously it had receded and become more welcoming, the last sanctuary in a dark hell, but now tragically out of reach. There was no turning back. She would find his body, or what was left of it, in the morning, when the last of night's scavengers had licked his bones and sucked out his eyes. He walked on toward certain death.

Safe inside the car, Celine watched Robert disappear entirely into the shade and the darkness as he approached the cabin. She was not afraid of the dark. Well, certainly, she was not afraid of normal darkness, like night in the city when the yellow glow of sodium light revealed all corners; or even of perfect hotel darkness, achieved with shutters and blinds but relieved at the flick of a switch. Country darkness was different, somehow malevolent. She locked the car doors, but she knew it would do no good because whatever monstrous creature of the night came for her, it would not bother with doors. Either, she knew, it would rip the roof off with its talons or, more likely, it would simply smash its face through the windshield before a giant prehensile tongue wrapped itself around her neck and pulled her toward a pair of jaws. If she were lucky Robert might find some shreds of bloody clothing in the morning, but no one would ever know the terror of her final seconds. Celine wished that after all that she had not made such a fuss about being cold.

Robert reached the cabin at last, surprised to have made the journey unmolested. He had his plan for the next stage of the operation all worked out. Stage one: knock at the door and wait. If it was answered by some strange backwoods huntsman with weird religious beliefs, a collection of skulls, and a scythe kept sharpened in readiness for Armageddon, then he (Robert) would make his excuses and back away. If there was no reply, he would move to stage two.

He heard the knock echo inside the hollow interior of the cabin. There was no reply.

Robert had never before broken into an isolated cabin chosen at random, or indeed anywhere else. This was new ground, but then never before had he been sacked, jilted, evicted, assaulted, and drawn into a kidnapping all within twenty-four hours, so the addition of one more novelty did not cause him much concern. Wrapping his jacket around his hand, he smashed a small pane of glass in the corner of a window. Carefully he snaked his arm through until he was able to release the catch. He drew his arm out again and with one firm pull he opened the window.

* * *

Back at the car, Celine had had enough of waiting to die. She could practically hear the great slobbering monster dragging its way toward her. She knew it would go for her, because she was young and female and therefore, according to convention, liable to scream, which was what it wanted. This she knew for certain. Thinking still further, she realized that what it wanted even more was for her to leave the very relative safety of the car and attempt a foolish and futile flight toward the cabin. Well, Celine was damned if she would give it the satisfaction.

She waited for fully thirty seconds. Then she opened the door, got out of the car, and ran toward the cabin, from which a bright light suddenly shone. She ran as though her life depended on it, surrounded as she was by the monsters of darkness.

The presence of a functioning electric light was the first of two surprises for Robert. The second was Celine's arrival, pale and breathless at the door of the cabin.

"What's the problem," he sneered as she slumped into an armchair. "Afraid of the dark?"

The place was furnished, but did not appear to be currently occupied. A simple vacation cabin, the perfect home and hideaway for Robert until he worked out his next move. At least up here he would get time to think. There was one bed. He looked at it with longing. His exhaustion demanded relief. He would sleep with the gun and the keys next to his skin. That way she could not steal them in the night.

But still, he realized, she could slip away at dawn, down the hill toward the road and the nearest town, freedom and the police. Worse still, she could approach him while he slept and dash his brains out with a saucepan or cut his throat with one of the kitchen knives. He wouldn't put it past her. By the time he had lit a fire, he knew what he was going to do.

"I'm going to tie you up."

In the absence of a rope (although later he found one), he tore a sheet into strips with which to tie her to the armchair. Hardly ideal, he knew, but the chair was deep and fairly comfortable. He would give her blankets and perhaps tomorrow he would think of something better.

She said nothing as he bound her wrists to the arms of the chair. She did not flinch as he pulled the knots tight. He felt slightly awkward and not a little repelled at treating his captive like this, but fatigue denied him any internal debate and drove him on to bind her securely.

Only as he fastened her legs with the cloth and found himself in uncomfortable proximity to her thighs, and still she said nothing, did he feel compelled to offer some explanation. "Let's get this clear," he told her, "I'm not going to hurt you. But this *is* a kidnapping."

She looked down at him. She was cool and unperturbed. Robert felt ridiculous, lurking between her knees like a useless voyeur.

"I'm the kidnapper, and you're the . . ." His voice faded out, unhappy at the inevitable conclusion.

"Victim." She said it for him.

"Yes. Victim," he said to show that he could say it, too. Reclaim the word, he thought. "That's the way it is."

"It's all right," said Celine, "I have been through this before."

Robert dropped the final strip of cloth.

"Kidnapped before?"

"I was twelve years old," Celine said.

"That's terrible," was all he could say.

"It was a long time ago," said Celine and sure enough to look at her you might have thought it was. The memory did not seem to generate much distress. It was she who looked relaxed, not Robert. A thought struck him.

"So how am I doing?"

"What?"

"How am I doing?"

"In the kidnap?"

"Yeah. In the kidnap. I just wondered, I mean you're experienced, right?" Robert looked at her, awaiting judgment and attempting to read her face.

Celine weighed his question. An honest reply didn't bear thinking about. "Well, so far you're not doing too bad."

"Hey, thanks." Robert stood back, flushed with relief. Not too bad. Under the circumstances, that was good. He was doing well. His morale cranked up a notch as he began to loop the final knot.

"Anyway, I'm just tying you up so you won't escape in the night."

"I know that."

"Of course, you would."

She delivered the bomb with casual curiosity. "Are you going to try to have sex with me?"

"No!"

"Isn't that what you brought me up here for?"

"No, it's not."

"It didn't even cross your mind?"

"No. Well." He thought about it—those uncomfortable inappropriate feelings as he tied her up, those suppressed inclinations.

"No," he lied.

"Do you have a problem with sex?" asked Celine, who had no problem making men feel as if they did have a problem with sex.

"No," said Robert, suddenly not so sure.

"Are you frightened of it?"

"Frightened?"

"Yes, frightened," she explained, "you know, by intimacy, performance, comparison, prowess—all that stuff."

"No. Of course not."

Celine let that pass. "Just nervous," she said.

"I'm not nervous!" shouted Robert.

"Then calm down."

"I'm perfectly calm!" he shouted again, more emphatically than was necessary he realized. "I'm just informing you," he continued, "that there is no sexual motive for my actions."

"I'm glad we've got that cleared up," Celine said with a friendly smile, as though they had just been discussing which was their favorite soap powder. Robert pulled the final knot tight and stood up.

"Why did you want me to shoot him?" he asked.

Celine paused then told him. "When I was twelve, they put a needle in my arm and took blood and sent it to my father. Next week they did the same, and then the same again until he paid up. He waited six weeks."

"I see," said Robert.

"Yes," Celine said, "that's what happens to the victim."

Despite his fatigue, Robert did not fall easily into sleep. His mind was troubled by all that he had gone through, by his crimes, and by the desperation of his situation. They could not stay here, wherever here was, indefinitely. He would need to formulate a new plan, but every attempt at rational thought was interrupted by the memory of women screaming at him as he held the gun in the elevator. He tried to remember the day before all this, but just as Lily's charms had faded from his memory, so, too, did the details of his previous life. It seemed he had no past, and when sleep came, late into the night, he dreamed again of a strange senseless ritual, still blurred and incomprehensible, wherein his life was threatened by forces of evil and saved by a figure unseen and unknown, but somehow familiar.

Celine's discomfort was more physical than mental. She had satisfied herself that her kidnapper was harmless, her final doubts having been settled by the interrogation that had so disturbed him. The day had begun badly, but ended well: She would not have to go to work, she was not in danger, and she was in a position to cause distress to her father. What more could she ask? The only problem was being tied to this chair, but tomorrow she would deal with that. And so she drifted off to sleep where she dreamed, as so often, of a twelve-year-old girl running through a dense forest at midnight, crying and screaming as she fled for safety, making her own escape from those monsters in the darkness.

10

With daylight, the idyllic location of the cabin was revealed. Behind it, jagged summits rose toward the sky. In the other direction, the tree-clad hills extended for mile after mile.

Leaving Celine tied up, Robert had made the short journey by car along the dirt track to the blacktop and then the three miles to the nearest hamlet, nothing more than a store, a gas station, and a bar serving the scattered rural community. And as he returned with two bags of groceries, walking the final fifty yards that had seemed so long the night before, he began to feel that things weren't really that bad. Okay, he shot Naville, and kidnapped his daughter, but a jury might understand. It was a first offense. Maybe they would just send him home.

Anyway, there was something invigorating about the wonder of nature, something about the thin clean air that made him glad to be alive. Look at me, he thought, I've got my health, my senses, why worry about tomorrow? He even had a companion, albeit one only present under duress and kept there by being tied to a chair, but a companion nevertheless. Singing to the world, he sprang up the steps to the porch and nudged the door open.

She was gone. The chair was still there, but she was gone. The pathetic strips of sheet were scattered on the floor and his companion had disappeared.

Robert's heart sank. He should have realized this would happen. The knots weren't tight enough. He had been too kind and this was how she repaid him, with betrayal at the first opportunity. Not only was he missing a companion now, he didn't even have a victim. She was probably miles away already and he didn't expect to see her again unless she was called as a witness to send him to the gas chamber or something similar. He certainly didn't expect to see her sitting in a corner by the broken window, reading a book, which is where she was when he snapped around to the sound of a turning page.

Celine did not look up.

She had wasted no time, as soon as Robert departed, in freeing herself from the knots, which she had already loosened in the night. She contemplated leaving, or escape, as it might be thought of, but did not feel inclined to do so on foot. She had no other plans or engagements for that day and besides, she was hungry and in need of coffee. To pass the time as she impatiently awaited Robert's return, she had settled down with a thick glitzy novel which she found in a drawer and read with ruthless speed.

Robert, fully recovered from his moment of apparent loss, placed the groceries on the table and approached Celine.

"Enjoying the book?" he asked.

"No," she replied, still without looking up.

"What's it about?"

"It's a romance," explained Celine. "This girl, she meets this guy. They fall in love."

Sounds good, thought Robert. Nice cover, too, he observed. *Games of Love*, embossed in gold, by Virilia Consuela.

"It's bullshit," said Celine.

Robert took a deep breath and bared his soul. "I'm planning to write a novel myself. Lots of people say that, but in my case it's true." He was not sure whether to explain the plot or not. There were still a few problems in the narrative that needed smoothing out, intricacies to be interwoven, that sort of thing. Perhaps now was not the time.

"I'm not interested," said Celine, "in you, or your novel or any other pathetic ambition that you might have to change your miserable mundane existence. I'm not interested."

Robert, suitably deflated, thought this over. As a companion, his victim was not shaping up at all well. But if that was how she wanted it—

"How much have you read?" he asked.

"Two hundred pages."

"Want a change of scene?"

"No."

"A little exercise?"

"No."

"You can't say no, it's not a part of the arrange-
ment."

"I want to read my book."

"You said it was bullshit."

"Doesn't mean I'm not enjoying it."

"You said you weren't."

"A girl can change her mind, can't she?" said
Celine, but Robert had already snatched the book
away. There would be no more discussion.

Celine had never split logs before. It was not easy.
The ax was heavier than it looked. The logs were
solid and distressingly plentiful. It did not take long
before her hands were raw and her shoulders ach-
ing. The initial device of imagining that each log
was the head of some odious tormentor sustained
her through the first twenty (her father featured
eight times, Elliot four, and Robert twice, the remainder being "miscellaneous"), but thereafter she
became increasingly fatigued and bitter. She cursed
Robert loudly, but he was not listening. Instead he
was immersed in the thick glitzy novel which, he
was glad to discover, was not at all the garbage Celine had described, but was in fact a good example
of the racy exciting style toward which he aspired.

"I'll be the judge of that," he said firmly,
closing his shiny leather briefcase and snap-
ping the gold lock into place. He checked his
handcrafted Swiss chronometer. "I've got a
flight to catch."

For a moment fury burned in her eyes
and her cheeks flushed with anger, but all

was extinguished by a single flash of his incandescent smile. She almost hated him for the power he so effortlessly exerted over her emotions, but the truth was that she loved him too much.

She traced a finger around the waist of his Italian designer suit, sensing his firm abdominal muscles through the crisp cotton of his tailored English shirt. Avoiding his cold, gloating gaze, she let her hand drift down toward the swelling of his passion below. She heard his breathing become shallow and a flicker of a smile played upon her lips as she meditated on the power she now held.

"Are you sure you want to catch that flight?"

And Robert read on while the ax swung through the air, cleaving yet another log.

Meanwhile, some two hundred miles away, in a dingy low-rent apartment, O'Reilly was also reading *Games of Love* by Virilia Consuela.

This was the moment for which she had waited so long. She gasped with surprise and delight as she sensed the firm exploratory pressure of his flesh.

Her mind filled with a thousand crazy images while the frisson of delight erupted between her thighs. In the hidden recesses of her pelvis, their bodies fused into one writhing mass of torrid sexual imperative.

She pulled him closer, deeper, unable to

stop. This indeed was perfect love: inexplicable, unpredictable, and absolutely beyond control.

"Do you think they're in love yet?" Jackson asked without removing his gaze from the television.

"No," replied O'Reilly and returned to the novel. She did not care for interruptions. This was research, about men and women, the whole damn thing. She had already devoured, to refresh her memory, the *Kama Sutra*, *The Joys of Sex*, *Grey's Anatomy*, *The Female Eunuch*, *The Second Sex*, *Iron John*, the screenplays for *Debbie Does Dallas* and *Seven Brides for Seven Brothers*, the *Holy Bible* (in Latin), *Don Juan*, *Romeo and Juliet*, a biography of Jimmy Hendrix, Masters & Johnson's original survey, and several back issues of *Hustler* magazine. But the bountiful world of the cheap romance was where she gained the most. No barometer, felt O'Reilly, was more sensitive to the needs and aspirations of men and women than the novel with a gold-embossed title.

This was the third novel in Virilia Consuela's oeuvre that O'Reilly had studied and it was every bit as useful as the other two, as indeed it should have been, since it was identical to them in all but the names of the characters, and even they were drawn from the same limited pool. But O'Reilly found it useful. Furthermore, she enjoyed it, for romance was her weakness. Her short life with its tragic conclusion had left her hard and inexpressive, but in the secret depths of her heart, she still believed with unaltered intensity in the beauty of love. It was a belief she did not often reveal. Gabriel had touched upon it, in an unguarded moment of sensitivity and he saw it as her greatest strength. It lent her commitment in her job, and combined with guile and ruthlessness, made her without any doubt his leading operative. But for O'Reilly, it was something to be hidden from view, and only let roam within her mind, as it did now, under the influence of Ms. Consuela's vivid prose.

Jackson did not read. He could not concentrate long enough. He was restless and bored and found only limited solace in the television. This morning he had watched a confessional program in which "Men Who Loved Their Best Friends' Employers' Mothers" had opened up to public scrutiny their tales of misery, joy, regret, and justification. Now he was watching a football game, which at least seemed to offer some fixed values. As a commercial break interrupted the game, he watched and made an entry in his diary.

Commercial: Tall man with mustache and reassuring manner offers one-stop divorce settlement for $250. Simply dial 1-800, etc.

Jackson did not know what this might signify. Possibly nothing, but he liked to keep a note in his diary anyway. He looked back through it. Nearly one hundred and twenty days of misery of one kind or another. And the last week had been terrible.

Tuesday, September 11th—chest pain. Attended physician. Cardiograph normal. $400.00.
　　Wednesday, September 12th—wishbone stuck in throat. Coughed blood.

Thursday, September 13th—ringing noise in left ear for four hours. Unbearable. OR not sympathetic. Advises scrape out ear with knife? Serious.

And so Jackson knew it would go on and on until the mission was complete, if it ever was complete. It was all so confusing nowadays. They had thought the sixties were weird, but that was just the start. The nineties were beyond understanding.

"If they were in love," he said, "we could go home."

"Uh-huh," said O'Reilly.

"I hate it down here."

"Uh-huh."

"I hate the air and I hate the food. And I hurt all over. I sweat in the heat and I ache in the cold. And look at this place. What a dump. Damp. Roaches. No air con. Why can't we stay some place decent?"

"Budget doesn't cover that."

"Exactly," said Jackson, "budget doesn't cover it and why not?"

It was a rhetorical question but O'Reilly answered. "You know those mysterious ways you keep hearing about, Jackson?"

"Yeah?"

"Well, this is one of them."

"Well, I remember the good old days, when all you had to do was introduce a man and a woman and nature did the rest. Doesn't work like that anymore. Men, women, it's all gone to shit."

But O'Reilly was not listening. She was lost in the *Games of Love*.

* * *

Sun set on the cabin. Logs, chopped earlier, burned in the stove and in the open fire. Celine, victim and lumberjack, watched her work go up in flames and waited, hungry while Robert thrashed about in the kitchen in the way that only a male cook really can, exuding confidence but producing nothing. At length, however, he emerged, walking toward a table with two plates held proudly aloft. With a flourish he laid one plate before Celine, and the other at the far end of the table. The steak had been grilled and was served with boiled potatoes, tomatoes, and mushrooms.

Robert sat down and cut immediately into his steak, rare and tender. He cut again, this time combining the succulent steak with a piece of potato and a mushroom all skewered onto his fork. The sensory pleasure annulled for moment all the discomfort and tribulations he had endured and it was only as he cut into the steak for a third time that he realized Celine was not eating. He chewed and swallowed before he spoke.

"Not hungry?"

"I don't eat red meat," said Celine.

"Well, you can eat the vegetables," Robert said in what he hoped was a constructive tone.

"But they've been on the same plate."

"So?"

"I'm not going to eat this."

Robert put down his knife and fork. He controlled himself.

"Do you eat fish?"

"Yes."

"And poultry?"

Celine nodded.

"But not red meat?"

"No. Or eggs. Unless I know they're free range."

The meal was over. The sensory pleasure that had soothed Robert was nothing but memory and they stared angrily along the length of the table at each other. Celine showed no sign of regret or compromise.

"Why didn't you tell me you don't like meat?"

"Because you didn't ask. And, as a matter of fact, I do like meat. I just don't eat it. Moral reasons, if you must know. Now if you had taken the time to inquire—"

"Why are you such a pain to be with?" Robert shouted, slapping the table.

"Because," Celine shouted in return, "you tied me to the chair all night. Because I'm the victim and you're the kidnapper, apparently."

"Meaning exactly what?"

"Kidnap for beginners, chapter one: Have you asked for a ransom yet? Check 'yes' or 'no.'" She sat back and folded her arms, a smug tilt to her head and a patronizingly innocent smile directed at Robert. She had made her point. In fact, she ate red meat without reservation, but hunger was a small price to pay for such a victory.

Robert glared impotently. Reply, he had none. Seeking a distraction, he returned to his meal, but the steak looked gray and the vegetables limp, and the food, as they say, turned to ashes in his mouth.

11

Celine slept well that night, free of both physical ties and the monsters of her dreams. Robert had been unable to face the indignity of tying her up again, preferring to take his chance that she might choose to escape, and not expecting to be very disappointed if she did. Kidnapping, as a pasttime, was rapidly shedding what little gloss it had shown at the outset. There were so many things for Robert to think about: location, nutrition, security, etc., that it was no wonder he had overlooked such trivia as a ransom. He lay awake on the couch, for Celine had taken the bed without any discussion, and contemplated the nature of his forthcoming demand in exchange for Celine's freedom. In truth he would almost have paid to be rid of her, but this did not seem to be an option now. It was not clear whether she would go, even if he could have paid her. It was not supposed to be like this, so far as he knew. He tried to work it out, but dawn arrived and he was none the wiser.

* * *

Celine had driven them into the nearby township after a breakfast eaten in silence, of coffee, museli, and muffins. Robert's attempts at conversation had met with no response. Celine remained sullen and mute even as they stood together in the limited space of the telephone booth. Robert dialed and waited for an answer. He would have preferred to leave Celine in the car, but she had demanded admission in return for the number of her father's direct line. Her presence was unsettling for Robert, who could not help but be aware of her critical gaze and physical proximity.

"Don't say a word," Robert said unnecessarily, "until I tell you to."

Celine sighed. A ransom demand, she knew, was an act of force and cunning. Nothing so far in Robert's behavior had convinced her that he was suited to the task. She could hear the ringing cease and the muffled sound of her father's voice, and then Robert began to speak.

"Hi, Mr. Naville. It's me. What? Look, I—yes, that's right. Me. Kidnapper. Yes. What? Well, no, it's not like that. That's unfair. Now—"

Celine depressed the cradle, cutting Robert off.

"What are you doing?" said Robert.

"No, what are you doing?"

"Negotiating with your father."

"Get very far?"

"He kept interrupting."

"Right."

"He wouldn't let me finish."

"Remember what they didn't teach you at Harvard Business School?"

"I didn't go—" began Robert.

"It's a figure of speech," said Celine.

"Oh."

" 'Negotiation is weakness.' Right? You're the kidnapper, remember that. You demand and he complies. You go in hard and you go in fast."

"Hard and fast," repeated Robert.

Celine took the receiver from his hand.

"I'm you, okay?" she said. "You grasp that? Now imagine it's ringing. You psyche yourself up. Grrr."

"Grrr."

"Right. He answers."

And then with no warning, Celine began shouting down the phone. "Now you fucking asshole, I've got your daughter here and I'm going to mail her back to you in pieces if I don't get what I want: I'm going to cut her fingers off with a pair of pliers and fry them up for breakfast." And then, equally abruptly, she reverted to her calm instructional manner. "And so on, like that, for no more than thirty seconds. What's the problem?"

Robert was staring, open-mouthed, not sure whether to be impressed or horrified. He did not need to ask where or when she had learned this approach, and he took the receiver without comment. He dialed again, but scarcely had he blurted out his first polite inquiry than she cut him off.

He tried again. And again. And again. Eventually, he wound himself up for a final effort. He looked into his dark side. He said, "Grrr," a few times. He clenched his jaw and he dialed.

Celine watched and listened as at last he got it right.

"Right, you arsehole"—Robert exuded fury—"I've got your daughter here and I'm going to mail her back to you—"

Robert gasped and slapped a hand over his face. "Sorry, madam, I must have dialed the wrong number."

Celine listened in disbelief as Robert continued.

"No, madam, I don't have your daughter, I have someone else's. No, we're not married. What? Yes, I've read that: finding suitable young men can be a problem." Robert relaxed again, evidently enjoying the relief of a normal conversation.

"Well, I'm sure your daughter is very nice. Yes, well, in principle I've no objection to meeting her but—Hey, what's the problem?"

She had cut him off again.

"Maybe you ought to just send a letter," Celine said, with a hint in her voice of something alien but unmistakable: the sound of jealousy.

Wanted: experienced person(s) to locate and retrieve valuable item lost under distressing circumstances. Rate paid according to expertise plus expenses.

Naville, like his daughter, was unimpressed by Robert's abortive attempt to extract a ransom. He had no intention of paying a cent to retrieve his daughter, a resolution that was merely reinforced by the blundering series of phone calls that had interrupted his morning's work. And interruptions to work always annoyed Naville. Being shot in the leg, apart from being painful and life threatening was an interruption to work. Being under anesthetic for two hours and in the hospital for three days was an interruption to work. For a man to whom time was money, this meant that Robert had already cost Naville a small fortune, to which the addition of a ransom was unthinkable.

Not that he was unwilling to spend money, for Naville was a firm believer that you only get what you pay for in life. The involvement of the police, for example, was not a service for which he would pay directly (or indirectly, given his propensity for tax avoidance) and therefore held no attraction for Naville. Privately employed detectives or bounty hunters, however, cost money and must therefore offer satisfaction in return, he reasoned. As a further complication, there were certain aspects of the task Naville had in mind at which the police or one of the larger detective agencies might express misgivings. Instead he had placed a small advertisement in a local newspaper and had sifted through the cranks, thieves, and fantasists who replied before selecting two who seemed at least moderately professional.

They sat in his office now, an odd team to look at: a big, tall, black guy with a wiry little white woman who did most of the talking. There was something about them that Naville had found impressive, though what it was he found hard to define. The woman spoke with a directness he warmed to, and they certainly seemed familiar with the type of work, but there was something else he liked, something familiar but he couldn't pin it down and let it drift to the back of his mind. He had explained the circumstances of his daughter's kidnapping (or at least his version), identifying Robert and describing the cold-blooded shooting. They had nodded as he emphasized the importance of his precious daughter, the apple of his eye, jewel in his crown, etc., being returned unharmed. Her safety was paramount, he had repeated, and they had responded, expressing confidence in their ability to do as he wished.

"You've done this kind of work before?" asked Naville.

"We do everything," said O'Reilly, "eviction and debt collection are our daily bread, but the personal retrieval, bounty hunting, you name it—we do it."

"How much?"

"Our fee for the recovery of your daughter is one hundred thousand dollars."

"That's a lot of money," said Naville, who had never lost sight of the fact that a dollar is a dollar is a dollar.

"Five thousand advance," said O'Reilly, "the rest cash on delivery. No daughter, no dough."

She sensed Jackson stirring beside her and hoped he would keep his big mouth shut. This was one of the trickiest moments of their mission. Blow it now and they were in trouble. But Jackson felt the urge to speak.

"Naturally, we'd operate on a sliding scale, whereby if we only bring back a part of your daughter, we only get part of the money."

"That's enough, Jackson," said O'Reilly.

"I mean," he continued, "if he's cut her ears off and we can't find them, we'll knock a couple of thousand off the tariff. More for a limb, obviously."

"Jackson!"

"Sorry."

"Mr. Naville, I don't think you need to worry. My partner is simply envisaging the worst-case scenario."

O'Reilly smiled reassuringly, but Naville was not really listening. He did not care very much whether Celine came back with or without her ears. She never listened to a word he said anyway, so deauriculation could hardly make things worse. He was, in any case, impatient to discuss something far more important.

"What about the kidnapper?" he asked.

"You want him, too? That's extra."

"What if he gets in the way?"

"We'll deal with that situation if it arises."

"What," asked Naville, "if I want him to get in the way?"

"Let us speak plainly, Mr. Naville," said O'Reilly, "you want we should kill him."

"Yes."

Jackson and O'Reilly went into conference. Both were furious. As Jackson saw it, O'Reilly was leading them into deep and uncharted waters. Killing or even pledging to kill was a ludicrous tactic: This mission was to bring two people together, not blow one of them apart. Violence was beyond their remit, and contrary to his personal code of conduct.

"I don't want to kill anyone," he whispered forcefully.

O'Reilly's perspective was equally clear.

"Listen, Jackson, if we don't get the job, someone else will. Do you like it down here?"

"That's not the point."

"Let me remind you old buddy: We're here for the duration. We must succeed, and in order to succeed, we must be prepared to use whatever methods are required. Do you understand me?"

She looked her partner in the eye. Jackson conceded the point. They turned back to Naville.

"Two hundred thousand dollars," said O'Reilly.

"Including expenses?" asked Naville.

"Including all expenses, except medical costs, for which you bear full and unlimited responsibility."

"Only for the duration of the contract," countered Naville, who enjoyed nothing more than crude bargaining.

"Naturally," said the woman.

"It's a deal.

Naville watched them leave, shown out by Mayhew, who had hovered discreetly in the corner of the office throughout the interview. Once again the woman stirred some memory within Naville: an elusive moment of sound, smell, and touch that vanished as swiftly as it had appeared. Naville relaxed—he was glad he had hired them.

Mayhew was less impressed. He doubted their mettle for killing. But as usual, he refrained from comment. After all, he was only the butler.

12

Celine lay on the bed, staring at the roof. With half her mind, she was attempting to count all its beams, planks, and struts, then to estimate their length and thickness and guess from this figure at the number of trees that must have been involved in its construction. With the other half of her mind, she had been trying to solve a puzzle of a different nature. She was not, she knew, given to extremes of emotions. On one day she might trace this back to witnessing the separation of her parents; on another to being an only child; on yet another to a diet rich in glutamic acid. Take your pick, it was purely a matter of conjecture. Anyway, extremes of emotion were not her stock-in-trade, so why, she wondered, had she stomped away from the telephone booth in such a sulk? She replayed it in her head and it was like watching someone else.

"Maybe you ought to just send a letter."

What had she meant by that? On one level, of course, it was easy: She was venting her frustration at both Robert and her father, the ineptitude of one and the brutality of the other. But that was not enough. Why had she become particularly annoyed by Robert's conversation with the wrong-number woman? Why had there been that twist in her voice? One hypothesis presented itself: Celine was living out the trajectory described in so many of Virilia Consuela's novels (a few more of which Celine had by now skimmed). Character A is routinely dismissive and disinterested in character B until character C, a dramatic foil, exhibits attraction to B, at which point A is shocked to find herself/himself suffused with a new, exciting, frightening emotion directed at B and ultimately identified as . . . something unspeakable. Celine rejected this hypothesis. Virilia Consuela's novels bore no relation to real life. This girl, she meets this guy. They fall in love. It's bullshit.

But no alternative explanation came forward. Celine focused instead entirely upon the roof above her. Twenty trees, she guessed, and tried to imagine how long it had taken them to grow, how many gallons of water, how many hours of sunlight, and she envied the trees, so clear of purpose, so immune to extremes of emotion.

Only a matter of yards away, but separated by a world of thought, Robert was seated at the table, disemboweling a newspaper. Celine's sulk and his conversation with the wrong-number woman were both of no concern to him. Since the phone booth fiasco, he had declined to discuss his plans, but allowed Celine to roam freely around the cabin. She had shown no inclination to escape so far, but Robert knew this could be just a ruse to ease her departure when its time arrived. He kept the keys to the car on his person at all times—at least she would not take that.

With regard to Naville, he had given up on his original plan to demand his job back, all charges dropped, and a reasonable sum in compensation for psychological distress. Instead, consigning himself to the life of a wanted man, he had decided to go for straight financial gain. Naville, he realized, was more likely to respect a straightforward pecuniary demand than any fiddly haggling over quality of life and self-respect. They had met only once and exchanged just those few words since, but Naville was clearly a man with no interest in Robert as a person, only as a kidnapper.

And so, with a stick of glue and a pair of scissors, Robert was transforming the foreign news section of the local paper into a ransom note. It was to be a brief note, but before long he had exhausted the foreign news and was obliged to move on to the life-style section in search of vowels, and then to the full-page car ads, which offered an unparalleled range of differently sized dollar signs. It was just as he stuck down one of the largest and most imposing of these, with a kind of fat-boy, hall-of-mirrors look to it that spoke of confidence and know-how, that there came a single sharp knock at the door of the cabin. Robert froze. He thought perhaps he had imagined it.

A second knock. He did not move. Perhaps they would go away.

A third followed.

Robert stood up, walked slowly to the door, and opened it.

A man stood close up, close enough for his fetid deer-breath and musty odor to reach Robert immediately. He was tall, heavy, and haggard. Several days' worth of stubble coated his chin. A long, oiled-cotton raincoat reached his ankles, where a pair of creased black leather boots took over. From the frayed sleeves of the coat, evidence of several more layers of jacket, sweater, and shirt protruded. Everything was smeared with mud and stained with dark visceral colors.

"Good afternoon."

His voice was surprisingly gentle.

"Hi," said Robert, forcing a smile.

"I'm Tod Johnson," said the man. "I live up the hill."

"Pleased to meet you," said Robert, and sensing that this might be an innocent social call, held out his hand. The man looked down at Robert's hand as though wondering what purpose it could possibly serve. Robert withdrew the offending limb as casually as he could.

"I see most things from up there," said Tod.

"Must be nice."

"Saw you arrive. Big car in the middle of the night."

"Right."

"Wondered: who's that?"

"Perfectly naturally question." Robert was drenched in sweat.

"So I asked Felix."

"Felix?" asked Robert, wondering whether this was an acronym for an FBI computer.

"Felix is my friend, but he's never been the same since the war."

"Of course."

"So I said, Felix, tell me, are they good or evil? One bark for good, and two for evil."

"Oh," said Robert, relief coursing through this body. "Felix is a dog."

The man's face assumed a fixed and ugly mask. He leaned forward and seemed to grow so that he loomed over Robert, who fought with his instinct to recoil from the stifling exhaled gas. It was the smell of something that might be dredged from the bottom of a swamp, having gone missing ten years earlier while hitching from coast to coast.

"You think I talk to a dog?" said Tod. His voice was calm. "You think I'd ask a dog whether you're good or evil? What do you think I am? Some sort of backwoods lunatic, with a barnful of human skulls and a scythe that I sharpen every day in readiness for Armageddon?"

He paused, awaiting a response.

Robert swallowed a lump of dry air before he spoke. "No, not at all. I'm sure you're a regular guy."

"Damn right I am," said Tod, no longer calm, spluttering into Robert's face, "and the point is: Who are you? Who are you?"

"Well, I'm—" began Robert but he did not know how to finish. A janitor? An immigrant? A regular guy? A victim of circumstance? A kidnapper?

"We're newlyweds," said Celine, opening the door.

Robert barely recognized her. Her hair was ruffled, a broad smile dominated her face, and what was she wearing? A sheet?

Tod gaped in open astonishment at the heavenly

creature who stood before him. With the white sheet wrapped around the curves of her form and held closed in front, she had an air of Olympian beauty. Tod surveyed her in awe from top to toe and watched the smooth line of her neck as she turned to Robert and spoke with a voice of sweet desire.

"Are you coming back to bed soon, darling?"

Robert did not know what to say, but fortunately the words formed themselves. "This is Mr. Johnson, dear."

"Pleased to meet you, ma'am."

"You may call me Lucille," said Celine and she extended a hand toward Tod, which he encased in his own scaley, callused paw. However, his grip was warm and gentle, and when he lowered his head to kiss, it was a brief and delicate contact he made.

"The pleasure's mine, Lucille," he said, standing straight.

"Are you from the newspapers?"

"No. I live up the hill."

"You mustn't tell the newspapers," said Celine with a conspiratorial air. "They never leave us alone. On account of Richie."

"Richie?"

"You recognize Richie, don't you?" said Celine, indicating Robert. "Richie Vanderlow: six gold albums, three platinum, and fourteen consecutive top-ten singles? Biggest-selling artist worldwide for the past twelve months."

Robert gave a smile and a modest shrug, relaxing against the door in casual mode. It was not exactly the dream bio he would have chosen for himself—no references to being a golfing prodigy, running with the bulls at Pamplona, or penning a series of bestselling novels—but it wasn't too bad all the same.

Tod now studied Robert with the same reverence he had for Celine. A struggle to remember was written on his face, but at length he shook his head and turned back to Celine.

"You have to understand, ma'am, that I watch mainly the Biblical channels."

"We were married in secret," said Celine, "in a castle in Scotland."

Tod seemed lost.

"That's in England," she added.

No closer.

"Near Paris."

"Ah, Paris," said Tod at last, with a knowing sway such as an accordion player might give as he wandered at midnight through the alleys of the Quartier Latin.

"It was very romantic—we stayed for our honeymoon, but it wasn't long enough so we came here for the sake of a little privacy."

"I see," said Tod, who did not.

Celine pulled the door open wide. "Would you like to come in?"

Tod did not move. He seemed fixed to the spot, staring ahead like a man in the grip of a sensation so intense that he can no longer tell whether it is pleasure or pain.

Robert and Celine waited.

"No," said Tod. "No. Thank you, but I'd better be on my way. I have to feed Felix."

"Pleasure to meet you, Mr. Johnson," Celine said as she turned and walked back toward the bedroom. Robert and Tod watched her go, the white sheet adhering closely to her skin. Robert turned to close the door. Tod backed away and his voice trailed off as he offered final counsel.

"You take care now, Richie."

But Richie was not listening.

Celine was dressed when she reappeared, composed instead of surprised, businesslike instead of flirtatious. Robert was not yet ready for such speedy transformations and greeted her with a smile.

"Thanks."

But Celine went straight for the table and picked up his handicraft.

"This?" she asked.

"Ransom note," said Robert, confident that she would approve his initiative.

"Anonymous?"

"Yes," he said, still confident, but aware of a certain hostility in her posture.

"Robert, my father knows who you are."

Robert blinked and turned away. "I didn't think of that." He despaired. It was so simple, yet he had managed to get it wrong again. He would have condemned himself, but she did it for him.

"You are the worst kidnapper I have ever met," said Celine flatly.

"That's what I am to you, is it? The latest kidnapper. A life-style accessory. If it doesn't work, well, it doesn't matter: You can always get another."

"Stop being so melodramatic."

"I'm trying to do my best here under difficult circumstances and it's not made any easier by you criticizing everything I do."

Celine had plenty more to say, but held her silence. So far, the kidnapping had been, in truth, a disaster. Diverting and painless, but still a disaster. She realized that Robert had almost reached breaking point and although texts on man management had never featured largely in her reading lists, she knew that further pressure at this point might not be constructive. If there was anything to be salvaged from this sorry affair, she must allow him his "space" to recover dignity and purpose and so forth. All this she told herself, although her instinct was to launch forth with an unstinting inventory of his faults and deficiencies.

She looked at the ransom note which read so far, in a range of type faces: *"I have your daughter. If you want to see her again it will cost you $ "*

"So how much are you asking for?" she asked.

"Half a million."

"Dollars?"

"Yes."

"U.S. dollars?" Celine said with genuine disbelief.

"Is there a problem?" Robert asked, awaiting the next assault with resignation.

"It's just that if word got around that I had been liberated for half a million dollars I could never show my face in polite society again. Diamonds have no value except that which is placed upon them."

Robert slumped down on the couch. "It's a lot more complicated than I thought." And he laughed a hollow laugh.

Celine sat down beside him. "I'm sorry," she said.

"It's all right."

"I shouldn't have got angry."

"I made an elementary error. It must be frustrating."

"You're trying hard and you're keen to learn. That's important," said Celine, and she meant it. "Just don't lose sight of the fact that we have an opportunity to make millions of dollars."

"We?"

"You and me, Robert. We need to work together."

"Isn't that a little irregular?"

"Yes, it is."

Robert thought it over. "I suppose it hasn't been a very good kidnap."

"Not a complete disaster."

"But not far off it. You don't need to say anything."

"It's just that neither of us is suited to these roles."

"Take a lot of strain out of the situation."

"Yeah."

They both fell silent for a moment.

"Millions?" said Robert.

"Millions," said Celine.

The first lesson was in the handling of a weapon.

"You stand like this," said Celine, blowing apart some assorted fruit from a distance of twenty feet. Birds fluttered away from the woodland clearing where she and Robert had set up their targets.

"With your arms out like this in front of you,"

she continued, "not like this, or like this." And she demonstrated the forbidden postures of a cowboy.

"Like this." She demonstrated once more before handing the gun carefully to Robert.

He held it as she had shown, recalling his only previous experience with a firearm: the shooting of her father. The gun did not feel comfortable in his hand. He squinted down the sight. The apple seemed miles away and the pumpkin scarcely any nearer.

Celine took his arm and raised it, kicking his feet slightly apart to improve his stance. "That's better," she said. "Now remember: never point a loaded gun at anyone unless you plan to kill them. Always keep the safety catch on unless you are about to fire. Wait until the last possible moment before firing: if they are more than a couple of yards away, you won't hit anything. Any questions?"

Robert shook his head. He tried to control his breathing and as he exhaled, he pulled the trigger. The recoil kicked his hands up. He fired a few more shots in quick succession.

He and Celine looked at the perfect unblemished fruit.

"Let's hope you don't need to use it."

Celine cooked that evening. Like driving, it was something she had never needed to learn, but she took to it with the same determined enthusiasm, and parts of the omelette were certainly edible, even if the outer surface had the appearance, texture, and taste of charcoal.

"Sorry," she said as Robert struggled with a lump of carbon and cheese.

"No, it's lovely."

"Now remember."

"Don't get caught."

"That's the main thing."

They had run through this several times, the plan for collecting the money, where to meet to divide it, the likely profile of whoever was representing her father, what they would do if they caught Robert (torture and murder), and what not to do under any circumstances (get caught).

"So what's the principal goal for tomorrow?" asked Celine.

"Collect the ransom?"

"No, the principal goal is not to get caught. So long as you don't get caught, you can try again."

"I see what you mean."

"I hope so. More omelette?"

Robert dreamed vividly again that night. It was the same semiamorphous dream in which his life was threatened before being saved by some shadowy figure. But now the details of the dream were taking shape. Perhaps the shooting practice had left its mark, for there was certainly gunfire in the dream, at the moment of his salvation. But stranger than the gunfire and preying far more on his thoughts the next day was another more crucial evolutionary step. It came as the dream was ending: the lights seemed to go up, the detail sharpened and just before he woke, he had seen the face of his savior, the shadowy figure, and on that face was a smile.

13

Celine was weeping as she screamed down the telephone, pleading with her father to pay the ransom, telling him that hideous death awaited her should any tricks be played. It was a gutsy, emotional performance, an off-Broadway classic, calculated to tug at the strings of all but the hardest of hearts, so what effect, if any, it might have on her father, Celine could not tell. Still, she had done her best, and after lunch Robert set off alone to the designated location where, it was hoped, he might collect the money.

Jackson made an entry in his diary.

> Long period of preparation over. Now in action again. Worried about use of violence. Hope no killing. O'R excellent shot, but plan v. complex and liable to human error. Also pain in left foot. Suspect gout or cancer but

O'R refuses to release funds from advance in order to consult physician. Much grumbling about *my* expenses as though hers are negligible. Have started counting cost of paperbacks, videos, reference books, etc. Total easily $200 plus already. Anyway, hope for success and speedy departure from miserable earthbound life.

He and O'Reilly had started their journey a few hours earlier than Robert, after a phone call from Naville. The game had begun, he told them, and he expected a trophy at the end. They drove in separate cars up into the hills to a section of straight road overlooked by rocky terrain. Here Jackson left his car, an old Chevrolet, and O'Reilly drove them up a steep winding track to a vantage point looking down along the road. And here they unpacked and waited.

It was midafternoon by the time Robert reached the road. His nervousness had grown steadily throughout the journey and he wished that he was not alone, that his life was simpler and he did not have to do this. He wondered about death and he hoped that Celine was wrong about the torture, although he suspected that she was not. She had told him about the fate of her previous kidnappers: Naville had eventually, after much blood, paid the ransom, then sent Mayhew off on a two-year trip around the globe to hunt down, torture, and exterminate each of the four men and anyone in their immediate entourage, which task Mayhew had undertaken with conspicuous ferocity.

Celine knew however that it would not be Mayhew this time. Twelve years had passed and the old soldier did not have the appetite for such adventures anymore. He had settled into a domestic role and showed no inclination to torture and kill. Furthermore, he had undergone some sort of spiritual experience and was now a practicing Buddhist. In his place, Celine had warned Robert, there would surely come someone equally potent and dangerous.

It was these thoughts that occupied Robert as he brought Naville's Lincoln to a halt some twenty yards from the Chevrolet. He stopped, waited, and looked around. There was no sign of any human presence, but he wished they had chosen somewhere less overlooked by tree and rock.

He checked the gun, as he had been shown, to be sure that it was loaded, the safety catch on, then got out of the car. He was unlikely to be killed at this moment, he told himself, since theoretically, if he was dead, they would never find Celine. First the money, then the girl. That was the deal. He walked to the Chevrolet, expecting the sudden appearance of a gun-wielding psychopath at any moment, but the car was empty, as arranged. He walked slowly round to the trunk. The money would be in there. It occurred to Robert that they might have placed a bomb inside, but again, this was unlikely. He opened the trunk.

Inside was a bomb.

Or at least it looked like a bomb. Brown paper surrounded the telltale contours of several sticks of dynamite, while wires led to a trigger device and a digital clock, that was even now subtracting silently from ten toward zero. Robert held his breath and closed his eyes. The end was coming. Running away would only transform a quick death into a slow one. He braced himself for the explosion that would scatter his remains far and wide, but after thirty seconds, still feeling alive and very much intact, he opened his eyes, breathed again and concluded that there had been no explosion.

He reached down and tugged at the wires. They came away, unconnected to anything. Next he lifted out the brown packet of dynamite and carefully peeled off the wrapping. Inside, instead of sticks of explosive, were ten large carrots. Apart from this, the trunk was empty. There was no money, not a single dime. Relief was mixed with disappointment and both were smothered by confusion. Robert bit into one of the carrots. As he did so, a sustained volley of automatic gunfire ripped into the Chevrolet, puncturing its tires and its fuel tank, punching holes in the doors and glass.

Robert threw himself into a ditch beside the road and crawled back toward the Lincoln. The bullets thudded into the ground behind him, but he remained unscathed. As he reached his own car and scrambled inside, the firing stopped. Reloading, he assumed, and wasted no time in starting the engine.

High up on the hillside, Jackson watched through binoculars as the Lincoln disappeared around the bend. O'Reilly was already dismantling the tripod and returning her rifle to its plastic cover.

"Nice work," he said.

"Thanks."

* * *

Robert had covered three miles before he first saw the other car, an Oldsmobile, in his rearview mirror. He couldn't see who was inside, but it was moving fast and he had no doubt that he was being pursued. He tried to accelerate ahead, but despite the Lincoln's heavy power, the Oldsmobile seemed to cling to the road around the twisting bends, and each time he saw it, it had drawn a little closer.

Robert almost killed the hitchhiker. Preoccupied by events in the mirror, he only saw him at the last moment. But even as he brought the car to a violent halt, he had devised a plan to complete his escape. It took only seconds to accomplish the switch and Robert hid in the trees by the side of the road while the hitchhiker sped away. The Oldsmobile passed by shortly after. Robert did not see the faces of his pursuers, but once satisfied that they were not returning, he set off in the opposite direction, on the long walk home.

A few miles farther on, the hitchhiker stood by the black Lincoln, waiting for Jackson and O'Reilly to arrive. He watched the Oldsmobile pull up and they both got out. Strange couple, he thought, and not for the first time. He had been sleeping on a bench in a public park when they had approached him, this tall black guy and the scrawny little white woman who did all the talking. Forty dollars, she said. All he had to do was drive a car. Plus he'd have to stop the car in the first place by standing in the middle of the road.

"What if I get killed?" he'd asked O'Reilly.

"You won't," she told him and gave him a ten-dollar advance. There was something certain in her manner—she knew she was right. And she was, all the way.

"No problem," he told her. "Exactly as you'd predicted. 'Quick, drive my car.'"

O'Reilly flipped open her wallet and drew out three creased bills.

"There's the balance."

The hitchhiker folded them carefully away.

"You can keep the car," she added, "but remember: It's stolen." She turned to walk away, but was interrupted.

"If you don't mind me asking," said the hitchhiker, "how did you know he would react like that?"

O'Reilly looked at him; he was fresh, inquisitive, young, and alive.

"It's our job to know things like that."

"But how?"

"We just know."

"Who are you guys? CIA? FBI?"

"That's not your concern," said O'Reilly with benevolent intention.

But the hitchhiker would not be thrown off. He had caught a scent of something weird, something he could not name. He had traveled around a bit, met plenty of cops, crazies, survivalists, would-be spooks, and embittered vets in bus stations and YMCAs all across America, but these two were not just different, they were alien. They exuded purpose and serenity, and they knew things, all sorts of things. It was a difficult question, but he had to ask.

"Are you . . . I mean, are you?"

O'Reilly was staring deeply into him—a stare that he had never experienced before. But it was Jackson who spoke, with a voice that was soft and humble.

"We're on a mission."

"Missionaries," said the hitchhiker, "that's cool."

They were close to him now and O'Reilly was smiling.

"So how do I join?"

"You want to work with us?"

"Yes."

"Tell him, Jackson."

"Well, first of all, you die," and Jackson stopped there.

O'Reilly waited before continuing, observing the hitchhiker's reaction as the words sank in. "First of all you die," she repeated, and thought back to one bleak dustbowl morning and a woman sitting in a wedding gown, crying. The woman is not in the first flush of youth, but the dress is white and rightly so. Life has been hard. It is hard for everyone in these times. She has cared for her parents with devotion unto their graves. Perhaps she has neglected her own life, or perhaps it has not been in her nature, but no partner did she find until last winter when a local merchant professed his affection. It is as though she is reborn. Strange, unaccustomed, beautiful feelings are with her in the morning as she wakes; in the evening when she lies down; and in dreams beyond. As spring comes, she feels that she too is green and full of life. Come summer the talk on their strolls by the river is of nuptial bliss and plans for their home together. He is not rich, but he runs a store and has a decent income. She has some savings and will help in the store. She is not too old to have children of her own.

With care and joy she plans the wedding. What few relatives she has will come. For weeks she has labored to make the dress. But this morning, she has received a message, carefully written on fine paper and delivered by the young boy who works in the store. Its words are chosen for their kindness, but brutal in effect. Three years now, he has known a woman, the wife of one of his customers. The man has died now, after a long illness, and he intends to marry the widow. It is final, for the widow is carrying his child. He is sure she will understand. He never intended to hurt her and wishes her well, but can he never see her again.

Her heart is broken. All is darkness. The timbers of her house burn fiercely that night, with her and her wedding dress at the center of the inferno.

All this O'Reilly recalled as she spoke. "You die wronged and betrayed in love, denied that spark of happiness, that blissful consummation—the communion of souls. You never know that joy because it was stolen from you, and so you spend eternity seeking to give others what you could not have yourself."

Jackson reached into his jacket and lifted out a revolver. He cocked it and held it to the hitchhiker's head.

"But first of all you die," he said.

"You still want to join?" O'Reilly asked. "All you need to do is say the word."

They knew, the hitchhiker realized, they knew

of his life, the string of insubstantial, transient affairs, the longing in his heart for something more. They knew that he was suited to their purpose. They had sought him out with such a role in mind, he realized, which indeed they had, for it was within the remit of all operatives to seek suitable recruits to the department. All he needed to do was say the word, but no, he was not ready. He still believed he would find love on earth. He shook his head, and Jackson lowered his gun.

O'Reilly was disappointed. She had liked the young man. He reminded her, in spite of herself, of someone she had known.

"Let's go," she said to Jackson.

14

Celine was irritated on two counts.

One. She was irritated with Robert for being so negative about the day's events. He had arrived back at the cabin fatigued, hungry, and monosyllabic. Only now, after sustenance and rest was he open to communication, but even this consisted mainly of her efforts to cheer him up. So unlike the works of Virilia Consuela, she felt, wherein it is the male who is the rock on which the brittle, emotional female finds security and support.

Two. She was irritated with herself for even thinking about the novels of Virilia Consuela which, she had resolved to believe, bore no resemblance to Real Life.

"Lighten up a little," she snapped.

"I was nearly killed today," said Robert.

"They weren't trying to kill you," explained Celine for the third time, "just trying to confuse and scare you."

"Yeah, before they killed me. And I lost the car

and I didn't get any money. Celine, I've had enough. I'm no good at this. I can't go on with it."

"So? You want to give up?"

"Yes."

"You think you can kidnap someone, then give up because you can't be bothered anymore."

"It's not like that."

"Kidnap is commitment, Robert."

"Now you tell me."

"You can't expect to get everything right the first time. Look, you're going to be fine. You're going to be a success."

The words were difficult, but she managed to get them out. Celine had never yet met a man who failed to respond to flattery if judiciously applied. Robert, she saw, was no exception. He sat up straight and looked at her.

"You think so?" he asked. Which, Celine knew from experience, meant: yes, tell me more.

"Yeah," she said, "you didn't get caught."

Which was true, and after all, it was what she had emphasized.

"No, I didn't," Robert said, looking on his deeds with a new perspective. "I fooled them, didn't I?"

"It was a neat trick," said Celine, almost meaning it. "I mean, it's a shame about the car but—"

"I got away."

"Sure did."

"Maybe we should go out."

"Out? Where?"

"To celebrate my escape. There's a bar in town. We could walk."

"Walk? I've never walked anywhere in my entire life."

"It's like jogging except slower, you'll love it. We'll go to the bar, have a drink, talk."

A strange realization was creeping up on Celine. It was not a part of her plan, yet was it totally unwelcome.

"Like a date?" she asked.

"Yeah," said Robert, "like a date."

The bar was more crowded than they had expected. Thursday night was Karaoke Night and from miles around farmers, loggers, automobile dealership owners, and men and women of no fixed occupation would gather to hear the classics of popular music delivered by their own. It was an opportunity for those who were gifted but unlucky to take center stage and reproduce the work of their heroes. And if those heroes could have heard, they would have trembled, for these shepherds and ploughmen, sons and daughters of toil, had voices of gold. Lives tarnished by disappointment and the unfulfilled promise of youth found expression in words so casually written, with phrasing and resonance that no professional, no star of stage or screen could ever match. Democracy has no finer symbol of its ideal nor any more eloquent reminder of its inadequacy than this simple amusement.

And in such an atmosphere of celebration and tears, Robert and Celine found a table in the corner farthest from the stage. A man with the look of a beaten dog was singing "Ruby Don't Take Your Love to Town," as though the words were etched on his soul while Robert recalled the conclusion of his life with Lily.

"I wouldn't say it was a bad relationship. No, Lily and I we had some great times together, we just, you know, grew apart as people. We were both very adult about it. There was no bitterness on either side."

"She left you," said Celine.

"No," said Robert, "no, no, no."

He thought it over. "Yes, she left me."

"The aerobics instructor?"

"Jesus, how did you know?"

"You have the demeanor of a man whose partner has left him for the aerobics instructor."

"I do?" Robert said, urgently scrutinizing, so far as he was able, his own demeanor. Christ, he thought all this time he had been walking around with a sign saying "dumb cuckold" stuck to his back, along with a "kick me" sign, of course.

"But be honest," said Celine, "it was inevitable. You were never suited to each other. You dream of something better, but she actually wants it now."

Robert nodded.

"Hence," she concluded, "the gymnast. Am I right?"

"Well, yes."

"It's a common scenario." Celine finished her beer.

Robert feeling curiously liberated by these forced revelations found himself emboldened and spoke without thinking. "Can I tell you about a dream I keep having?"

"No," said Celine.

"I think you're in it."

"I'm in your dream?"

"Yes."

"Oh, no."

She closed her eyes and rested her forehead against her hand. She recalled a boyfriend in her teenage years who had insisted on relating to Celine every detail of his juvenile, hormonally disordered dreams, frequently involving her head attached to the body of some other human or animal, or sudden gender alterations in midintercourse. This had been the young man's plan to bring sex harmlessly onto the agenda of their dialogue and hence facilitate its arrival into their relationship. The plan was flawed of course, facilitating only his departure from her life.

"It's not like that, I promise," said Robert, wishing that he had been less emboldened.

"I still don't want to hear about it."

"Okay."

"Good."

"It may not even have been you."

"Robert!"

"Sorry, I didn't mean to upset you. I know, I'll tell you about my novel."

She opened her eyes and laughed. "You're really writing a novel?"

"Yes, I've written a first draft," he lied.

"Uh-huh?"

"In here, at least." And he tapped his head. "I'll tell you about it. It's pretty good."

"I'm really not interested," said Celine as their waitress arrived with the cargo they had ordered. Celine set out the twelve small glasses in two rows and began to fill them from the bottle of tequila. Robert, undeterred by Celine's disinterest, pitched his novel once again.

"Nineteen-sixty-two. Marilyn Monroe is giving birth to baby girl, attended only by an elderly native American woman, and at the same time she is on the phone to JFK. It's yours, Jack, it's yours, she's saying. Right? Next, he's on the telephone to Mr. Fixer: fix it. The elderly native American woman takes a bullet in the head while Marilyn is murdered with a slug of barbiturate. Mr. Fixer is supposed to kill the child also, but in a moment of compassion, he takes it to an orphanage."

Celine had finished pouring. "So," she said, "the orphan grows up. Rich, beautiful, successful. Solves mystery and unravels riddle of own identity. Ad lib to fade."

"Well, yes," said Robert, "that's the bones of it."

"It's kinda obvious."

"The real work is in the telling."

"I'm sure it is," said Celine graciously. "Now listen, if I win, I'm free."

"Win what?"

Celine indicated the two rows of glasses, with salt and lemon arranged in between.

"It's a race?"

"If I win: I'm free."

"You're free already. I'm no more a kidnapper than I am Richie Vanderlow."

Celine was patient but resolute. "Indulge me, Robert."

"All right, if that's what you want."

"It's all I ever want," she said, slow and clear.

"I'll try to remember that."

Celine was on to her second before Robert's first glass hit the table. A life of hedonism and competitive self-destructiveness amongst the decadent and dying of the supersonic set was always an advantage in a situation such as this. Her dexterity and rhythm with salt, lemon, and alcohol were a wonder to behold. By the time Robert reached number four, she was sitting back, arms folded, a picture of victory.

"You're free," said Robert.

"That's right."

"Aren't you going to leave?"

He clenched his jaw. There was fire in his stomach and his mouth had just been rinsed with a vat of industrial solvent. Celine was less visibly distressed. Only a sheen across her forehead bore witness to her feat of consumption.

"We haven't got our money yet," she told him.

They both smiled. The burn was fading to be replaced by a warm glow as the tequila oozed into their blood and dilated their veins. Soon, an agreeable fuzziness began to pervade their brains, filling them with generosity and optimism.

Up on the stage, Ruby was asked for the last time not to take her love to town, but instead, for God's sake, turn around. The beaten dog was ushered from the stage to empathic applause and a familiar voice caught Robert's attention.

"Big hand there for local boy Scott Sherman."

Robert turned to face the stage just in time to see the bulky, unkempt figure of Tod Johnson point in his direction.

"And now it is our privilege tonight," said Tod, "to be joined by a very special guest and personal friend of mine, and I'm going to ask him to sing for us. Ladies and gentlemen, please welcome the biggest selling artist in the world with ten gold albums, six platinum, and fourteen consecutive number-one singles, Mr. Richie Vanderlow."

Robert found himself staring into a spotlight and was propelled by many hands toward the stage.

Tod shook his right hand and thrust a microphone into the left. Robert faced the crowd. A hushed expectation had replaced the hysteria.

"I've never even heard of him," said one man loudly, rapidly silenced by those around him. From underneath the pool table, where he lay curled on his side, a tall thin man gave three sharp barks.

"Hi," said Robert. He did not want to antagonize these people. "I'm Rob—Richie, I'm Richie Vanderlow."

There was a ripple of applause; Robert relaxed a little.

"I'd like to sing a song."

There was more applause and he grew in confidence.

"I'd like to sing it as a duet with my beautiful wife, Lucille."

A mighty cheer went up and the same hands propeled the reluctant Celine to join him. Robert looked at the monitor to check the title; he knew it vaguely.

"It's a special song for us."

Their blood was now substantially alcohol. Added to this, the room was hot, the lights bright and the atmosphere conducive to emotion. The song was a classic, a celebration of the durability and strength of love, from the point of view of one who has, through his own folly, lost his lover but finds himself unable to forget and tormented by regret. There are lots of things he wishes he had said or done, but he acknowledges that he never set aside sufficient quality time. Despite this failing, he is at pains to point out that he was always thinking about her. It was a cautionary tale designed to focus the hearts and minds of those who heard it upon their own relationships, to examine their own level of communication and physical intimacy. The wording of the song, it must be stressed, was more poetic than the above, but that was the general drift.

Robert and Celine sang with fervor and passion, to which the song lent itself greatly. Their audience wept openly and cheered as the song reached its gut-wrenching, spine-tingling coda, at which moment the night dissolved for Robert into a mysterious fragmented haze.

It was late morning when he awoke, startled to find himself lying in bed looking up at Celine. She was seated on the side in a blue bathrobe.

"Good morning."

"Oh God," said Robert, "what happened?"

"You were great," said Celine.

"I was?" said Robert, not sure exactly what she was referring to. She walked away to the living room.

Robert lay back and tried to piece it all together, with only limited success. He remembered the bar, the drinking, and then . . . not much. Singing? Had there been singing? And then there was that strange feeling of danger and salvation. He felt like he'd done all that before. Of course: It was the dream, just the dream, the same as every other time. But what about that other bit, the bit with Celine, where they sweated and held and heaved and fell exhausted into sleep? Was that also a dream? He lay naked under the quilt. His clothes were folded neatly beside the bed.

Great? Great at what, he wondered. He did not remember much and only one thing for sure.

"I remember drinking tequila."

"It was certainly a feature of the evening," said Celine.

"Then I had this really weird dream. It's the one I've had before. You're definitely in it now."

"I don't want to hear about it."

Robert got out of bed and wrapped himself in the quilt. Its warmth drew him back to his dream.

"We were on a game show called *Perfect Love*."

"I've never seen it."

"It's just a dream," said Robert, avoiding sudden movements as he transferred himself slowly. "I don't think the fact that it's a game show has any relevance. It merely indicates my cultural origins. Were I a tribesman from the Kalahari, the location would undoubtedly have been different, but the theme is universal."

Celine was waiting for him at the table. In front of her was a small soup bowl, a piece of paper, and a thin stick. In her right hand, Robert saw something sharp catch the light.

"Anyway, we were on *Perfect Love*, right, and my life was in danger."

"Are you ready?" Celine asked.

"For what?"

"To write a letter."

She drew the razor blade across her forearm in

a single confident stroke. At first there appeared to be no mark, then a thin line of dark blood began to ooze freely from the gash. Celine held her arm out to let the blood drip into the glazed curve of the bowl.

Robert struggled to maintain consciousness. Like most young men, he coped poorly with needles, blades, and blood. When a small pool had formed, he gave up the struggle and faded again into oblivion, disturbing Celine with the harsh thud of his head slapping against the floorboards.

Several days later, O'Reilly dropped a single sheet of paper, encased in a plastic cover, onto Naville's desk.

"Perhaps you'd like to keep this."

"Without our help," added Jackson, "that could be the last trace of your daughter you ever see."

Naville looked at the letter. They had some nerve. They had promised results, then come back empty handed, telling him that their quarry was "smarter than he looked" and "too dangerous to fool around with." Now this: a new and more outrageous demand. Control was slipping from his grasp. Naville knew about kidnappings: Never let your enemy set the agenda. Keep the pressure on. Deny them time and space. All these rules were being discarded one by one. He knew he should fire them and hire someone new. Spend more money. That was usually the answer. He could sense Mayhew's critical presence behind him, urging him silently to get rid of these two and ask him, Mayhew, for advice. Well fuck him, he was past it, had lost it, gone to worship Buddha. Naville would rather fucking die than ask Mayhew for advice. After all, he was only the butler.

Anyway, Naville did not want to fire Jackson and O'Reilly. There was still something about them, especially O'Reilly, that stirred some precious memory, like the echo of a melody he could not yet identify. And if he fired them now, he would never hear it again.

O'Reilly pointed at the letter. "We had it analyzed: It's his handwriting and her blood. He wants to make it a straight switch with no delay. He takes the money and he hands her back all in one."

Naville paused. He had the money in a suitcase at his side. He had already decided, but from behind him came a voice.

"With all due respect, sir."

"Shut up Mayhew. No one's asking you."

"Very good, sir."

And Mayhew stood back again, glowering at those two incompetents before him. It was not age that held him back, he told himself, it was Buddha. Pacifism was a central tenet of his new faith, not easy for a man who has lived by the sword, exceedingly difficult at times like this, but he held his counsel.

"He's an Aquarius, Mr. Naville," said Jackson.

"So what?"

"And your daughter's a Gemini?"

"Yes."

"From our point of view that's a highly adverse combination. Anything could happen." Mayhew snorted derisively. Naville ignored him. "I want her back."

"Don't worry," said O'Reilly, "we'll get her."

"And I want him dead."

"That's understood, too."

"Good."

Naville slid the heavy suitcase toward Jackson. As Jackson reached to take the handle, Naville clasped his hand around it.

"When it's over," he snarled, "I want this back."

No further words were exchanged. Jackson lifted the suitcase, and he and O'Reilly left the room. Naville watched her go, a three-note sequence playing over and over in his head.

The elevator was empty when they got in, but as Jackson and O'Reilly traveled down from Naville's office, it quickly filled and soon they found themselves crushed toward the back. Jackson's mind was racing. This was an opportunity he had long craved. Some might see it as justice, divine providence even. Proof that the Almighty does take care of His flock. He and O'Reilly had been sent to Earth on a miserable budget, nothing practically, scraping together nickels to buy discount food, and now here they were in actual bodily possession of a fortune. Jackson had been poor all his life and all his death, too. Poverty, he had discovered to his dismay on reaching the other side, was still regarded as good for the soul. In their zealous campaign to prevent any combination of men, needles, and camels, the authorities had found it convenient to make everyone poor, so Jackson, expecting nirvana, had found himself living in the astral equivalent of Poland circa 1950. Now, perhaps all that was about to change. There was only one catch: They'd have to fail.

"There's a lot of money in this suitcase."

"Don't even think about it," said O'Reilly.

"Just trying to work out what happens if we fail in our mission."

"If we fail in our mission, then we never leave this life, we never grow any older and we never die. We just suffer the indignity and decrepitude of flesh forevermore."

A few heads turned to watch the debate.

"And how can we alleviate that indignity?" asked Jackson. "Money." He slapped the suitcase to make his point. A murmur of approval went around. "I mean let's suppose we're in the situation where we're about to kill the guy, and the girl lets it happen. That's failure. What do we do then?"

Their audience awaited O'Reilly's reply to this dilemma. It was not helpful.

"We respond to the situation as it arises at the time. Go with the flow. Fuck it, Jackson, I don't know. In that situation we'll just have to improvise. Okay?"

The elevator reached ground level, but O'Reilly was not finished. "In addition, soldier, we are not going to fail. We have selected jeopardy as the tie with which we shall bind that young couple together, and when we're finished, nothing, but nothing will tear them apart."

She dipped her shoulder and pushed her way through the crush, followed by Jackson.

Those who had listened stood and watched, none daring to speculate aloud on the nature or meaning of this exchange.

15

❧

The vehicles passed at the rate of roughly one every twenty minutes for two hours. None had stopped but this did not bother them, for the day was warm and sunny, and the vista was hypnotic in its beauty. Rolling hills, covered in trees now turning all shades of yellow, brown, and gold extended as far as they could see. In such a pleasant setting Celine and Robert, a coiled rope draped over one of his shoulders, had walked along the lonely winding highway unperturbed by their failure to attract a car. This was a day they had anticipated with both joy and some unspoken sadness. For today they should collect the ransom. In doing so, however, Robert must also hand Celine over to her father's agents. They would meet up again, of course, weeks or months later, when it was judged safe, so that Celine could collect her share, but this day was the end of a certain period of their lives. When they met again, in a different place with different pressures and expectations, who could say what would happen. It was an issue they had chosen to avoid.

After the night of tequila, they had settled into a relationship of comfort and equality. They enjoyed each other's company and found delight in their isolation, fantasizing as they lay in bed at night that all this might never come to an end, that they might live out their days in rural bliss like two characters in a novel by Ms. Consuela. But fantasy they knew it was, for their lives followed separate paths, only crossing here before diverging again. This was known but unsaid.

They spoke of many things, mainly inconsequential. Robert told of the day it all went wrong: being fired, Lily and the aerobics instructor, the robot, and so on. Celine described the terrible threat of work that her father had wielded. Her romantic history, she had refused to divulge until this day, when she felt he might as well know. She had begun at the start, with the sexually confused adolescent, and moved on through the other juvenile suitors and fleeting attachments before she reached her first affair of substance.

"Bradley was nice: extremely wealthy, honorable, amusing, and generous."

"And?" said Robert.

"Eight-seven years old."

"Really?"

"He was healthy for his age."

"I see."

"His parents didn't like me."

"Pity."

"Then there was Jake. Nice guy: very rich but so conventional."

"Rich guys. Conventional. It's a problem," said Robert as though it was one he had experienced himself.

"And then there was Angelo. Twenty-five years old, handsome, healthy, exciting, sophisticated, and considerate."

Robert couldn't see a chink in Angelo's armor. He waited, but Celine said nothing.

"So?"

"So we grew apart as people. That's all."

He understood. "The aerobics instructor?"

"Like I said, it's a common scenario."

Robert swaggered to a halt. They could hear a car approaching.

"You hide," said Celine, "and I'll stop it."

Robert retreated behind the foliage while Celine stood at the roadside.

"So what happened next?" he called out.

"Well then I started to get problems with my teeth."

The vehicle was in sight now. A four-door pick-up truck. There were two men inside wearing baseball caps. Celine raised a hand and switched on her most luminous smile.

"Your teeth?" said Robert.

The driver of the pickup did not go through a lot of mental turmoil deciding whether or not to stop for Celine. It was a spinal reflex: As soon as he saw her face, his right foot fell hard upon the brake, drawing the truck to a halt right beside her. He and his passenger exchanged looks.

"Good morning, miss," said the driver.

"What you doing out here all on your own-
some?" added the passenger. "You want to step inside, we'll take you where you want to go, if you
get my meaning." He tilted his cap forward and
licked his lips.

"Plenty of room on the backseat, I reckon."

Celine simpered a little and they giggled with
joy. Then she pulled out the gun. They stopped gig-
gling. Oh God, they thought as one, crazy-female-
hitcher-with-gun scenario. Every redneck's night-
mare.

"Now," said Celine, as Robert emerged behind
her, "we're not stealing your truck: We're just bor-
rowing it."

In years to come the two rednecks would tell of
their lucky escape from the avenging she-beast siren
of the highways and her deviant male sidekick. Not
only had they not been emasculated, they had not
even been forced to engage in humiliating and un-
manly acts. All they had lost was their truck: A
small enough price for a man to keep his dignity.

Two hours later and sixty miles away, the truck was
stopped, engine still running, on a straight, flat
stretch of road, with open grassland on either side.
At either end of this stretch, about half a mile in
each direction, the road curved in through trees. But
at this point, there was little cover for a man or a
woman with a rifle. Behind the truck the rope that
Robert had carried lay straight along the road for
thirty yards. With a short piece cut from it, Robert

was binding Celine's hands. He performed the task carefully, tying tightly enough to convince, but not enough to hurt. He knew that time was running out, but there was something he had to say.

"Guess what."

"What?"

"I had that dream again, last night."

"Oh yeah."

"We're on a game show, *Perfect Love*, right?"

"Fascinating."

"My life was in danger."

"On a game show?"

"It's difficult to explain. Strange things were happening."

"So it would appear."

"My life was in danger, but you saved it. My heart was beating so fast, and then it stopped and my life was about to end. But you saved it, you saved my life."

He had more to say but his time had run out. The Oldsmobile appeared around the bend and he watched it stop at the far end of the rope. There was only one person in it, a tall man who got out of the car and lifted a large suitcase from the backseat. Robert stared, convinced that he recognized him, but equally sure that he must be wrong. It was so unlikely.

"Well," shouted Jackson, "what are we waiting for? Do you want to get on with this or not?"

"Sure. Right now," Robert shouted back. He drew the gun from his jacket.

"Send the girl over."

"First the money, that's the deal."

"Are you all right, Miss Naville?"

"I'm fine," said Celine, "just a little frightened."

"Don't you worry," said Jackson, "it's going to be okay."

Jackson tied the end of the rope to the suitcase and Robert began to haul it in. He was rather proud of this method of exchange. He wished now that he had chosen a more complex variant involving a bridge, with the money being hauled up from below to render pursuit even more difficult. But so far, this was working. He pulled the suitcase the last few feet along the road and flicked it open. He had never seen so much money, or even imagined it in any detail. He inhaled sharply.

"Well," said Celine, not looking down.

"It's here," said Robert, standing up.

"Okay, now send the girl over."

Robert and Celine looked at each other for the last time before they parted company, their paths already diverging. Their final words were mundane and practical.

"Be careful," said Celine, "and remember: don't get caught."

"Don't worry, I won't."

Celine began to walk across no-man's land toward Jackson.

"Shit," said Jackson to himself. This was not supposed to happen. They were supposed to be a couple now, to take the money and run together. Delivering the girl back to her father was not the plan. O'Reilly would not be happy.

Suddenly Robert fired in the air. Celine veered to the side of the road and Robert fired a series of shots in the general direction of the Oldsmobile, puncturing the body, one tire, and the radiator.

Jackson dived to the side of road, grazing his hands and knees on the gravel as he landed.

Satisfied with the results of his blitz, Robert jumped into the truck and accelerated away toward the curve in the road. He looked in the mirror: all clear.

Jackson picked himself up from the road. He was angry. Their plan did not appear to have worked and there was the girl to prove it. In addition, he had little bits of gravel stuck into the skin of his hands, and Robert had shot up the car and taken the money, and O'Reilly would probably blame him. So it was with a lack of grace that he lifted a shovel from the trunk of the car and, ushering Celine ahead, began walking in the direction of Robert's departure.

Further ahead, Robert had rounded the bend and two more before he was forced to break. There was a human being lying on the road, apparently dead, certainly motionless, her face turned down. She looked like a bit of road kill. There were no tire marks, no bloodstains, no scattered belongings to confirm this impression, but what else could she be doing there?

Robert waited for a moment. If she was dead, then there was nothing he could do. Maybe he'd phone the authorities later on. Best not to touch her in that case. If she was barely alive, then perhaps it was still best not to touch her. There was no reason to stop and get out. But what, he wondered, if she was not dead and not salvageable, but fatally wounded and about to die? If he drove away now, she would die alone. Damn it.

He opened the door and stepped down from the cab. He walked toward the prone form and knelt beside her. There was no movement of her chest. Robert felt relieved: Perhaps she was dead after all. He turned her over, bracing himself for the sight of horrific injuries.

"Don't move a fucking muscle," said O'Reilly, jamming her automatic pistol under Robert's chin.

He recognized her immediately. The Firm But Fair Collection and Eviction Agency. With violence or without, it's up to you. What the hell was going on here?

She reached inside his jacket and took his gun just as Jackson arrived at the scene, with Celine following behind, her wrists still bound together.

"What took you?" said O'Reilly, standing up and brushing the dust from her clothes.

"He shot up our car," Jackson said to focus attention on Robert.

"He shot up our car. What did you do that for?" O'Reilly nudged the barrel of her gun against his temple.

"I was trying to make a getaway."

"Trying to make a getaway," O'Reilly mimicked him, "fucking asshole." And she jabbed him sharply with the gun.

Jackson bent over and whispered in her ear. "It hasn't worked. They're not . . . you know. He let her go just like that. Didn't try to keep her and she didn't try to stay. We've lost, O'Reilly."

O'Reilly looked at them. Robert was still kneeling, while Celine watched him from several feet away, her disapproval clearly evident.

"What are we going to do?" asked her partner.

"Plan B, Jackson."

"Plan B. Oh God."

"Jeopardy, Jackson. It always works."

"I don't know."

"You got the shovel, Jackson. You can improvise the rest."

Under other circumstances the walk into the forest might have been a pleasant stroll. On either side of Robert and Jackson, virgin woodland extended for miles. Wild flowers grew in the long grass that sprang up wherever the sunlight forced its way through between larch, birch, and pine. But Jackson carried the spade and Robert, walking a few paces ahead, did not need to ask why. He toyed with the idea of trying to escape, zigzagging ahead through the trees, but Jackson's gun was drawn and Robert knew he wouldn't make six feet before being shot in the back. They had walked about two hundred yards before they came across a circular clearing about fifteen feet in diameter. Robert stopped instinctively: He knew that this would be the place. Surrounded by tall trees, their tops swaying in the breeze, it had the air of a sacrificial pit.

Jackson threw the spade onto the ground at Robert's feet. Robert looked down at it, then back at Jackson.

"You're going to kill me."

"That's right," said Jackson, returning his stare.

"Then I don't see why I should dig."

Jackson shrugged. It was a fair point. His reply was chilling and persuasive.

"If you dig," he said, "then when the time comes, I promise I'll shoot you through the head. If you don't like that, I can shoot you in the testicles right now and you can bleed to death while I dig the grave."

Robert started digging.

O'Reilly leaned against the truck. Ten minutes had elapsed and there had been no gunfire. What was Jackson doing in there? She started to think about what they would do with an eternity on earth, now that they had failed in their mission, for fail they certainly had. The guy let her go in exchange for the money, they didn't even speak to each other at the roadside, and then she showed no signs of emotion as Jackson marched him into the forest toward certain death. The girl was tough. O'Reilly could see that, and no wonder, considering what her parents had put her through. Perhaps it had been a mistake to expect her to fall for this kind of guy. At least they had tried: Gabriel would know they had tried, even if he condemned them to life on earth. And at least they would not be poor, now that they had Naville's money. They would need to invest it carefully of course; they had a long time ahead of them.

"Can you cut me free?"

It was Celine, holding her bound wrists out toward O'Reilly. O'Reilly paused. Perhaps it was an innocent request, perhaps not. In O'Reilly's experience, live human beings were best given as little freedom as possible. In fact, freedom was their curse. If only she had the power to be a little more direct, they wouldn't have all these problems in the first place.

The girl was persistent. "Please."

O'Reilly lifted from her pocket a large switch-blade.

"What's he going to do to him?"

"Shoot him in the back of the head, I guess," O'Reilly said with a provocative harshness.

"Right," said Celine, idle curiosity apparently satisfied.

"Would that be a problem for you?"

"No," said Celine.

Tough kid, thought O'Reilly, and she flicked open the knife, severing the strands of rope.

Jackson watched Robert dig. He, too, was troubled by their failure, by the prospect of an eternity on earth, with all its attendant miseries, and by the possibility that the Department had made a mistake. But his disquiet on this last score was not procedural, as it was for O'Reilly, but metaphysical. The Department was created by an omnipotent being. The Department was, therefore, within the limits of its role, also omnipotent. But somewhere along the line, the elements of choice and free will, so attractive in theory yet so damaging in practice, had been created and had caused all these problems for people like himself and O'Reilly. Now was it possible, Jackson wondered, for choice and free will to be controlled? In which case, they were nothing but a cruel trick on those who believed in them, or could an omnipotent being create something that would make him or her or whatever no longer omnipotent? And if he or she or whatever did that, didn't that kind of undermine their position in the universe? It was a frightening thought for Jackson who, like O'Reilly, would have preferred the continuous application of coercion and authority to all living things. That way, he believed everyone would be happier, even if they didn't know it, because they'd never have the chance or the inclination to find out otherwise. Kind of like communism, he reflected. Perhaps that was the answer, not more choice but less.

"Have you ever felt that you are not in control of events?" he asked Robert.

"Yes," replied Robert, feeling no need to add that his present situation was a more than adequate demonstration of just such a problem.

"No, I mean, when something is destined to happen, but it doesn't?" Jackson was at the heart of his argument now. "What happens if the forces of destiny are no longer in control?"

Robert stopped digging. Despite his imminent death, he felt sorry for this man in his despair. "I don't know," he told him. "Perhaps no one knows."

But this just seemed to make matters worse.

"Exactly, exactly," cried Jackson, "that's the whole point."

"Is it?" Robert asked.

"The truth is I don't think even He knows what's going down here. The mess. The chaos. The hatred."

"Who are you talking about?"

The man had really lost it now. Robert prepared

to drop the spade and run, but Jackson regained his composure.

"Just dig."

O'Reilly consulted her watch again. What the fuck was going on? She wanted to hear a single gunshot and then get moving. They had to drop Celine and get themselves someplace where Naville would never find them. That was the only option now.

For Robert, she felt no particular pity. When he died, he would become one of them, that was his fate and she could think of worse. Like life on earth, for instance. What a bum mission this had been. Jackson was right to complain: inadequate funding, no special powers, no chance of success, and no way out. How many years had she given the Department and what did it all amount to? Nothing.

"What are they doing in there?" she asked no one in particular. "I should have shot him myself."

"You can't trust them to do anything," said Celine. Together they looked into the forest.

"I take it you're not in a love situation," said O'Reilly.

"A what?"

O'Reilly always found this difficult, for despite her detailed research, the discussion of intimate emotions always flustered and embarrassed her. "I mean you're not 'in love.' "

"What is it to you?"

"Nothing. Nothing at all. Just asking," said O'Reilly, turning away to hide the color that ran to her cheeks.

Celine had not noticed O'Reilly's embarrassment, but this was the moment she had been waiting for. Her father, as she had predicted, had arranged for Robert to be murdered. Who knew what hideous tortures might already be underway in the depths of the forest? She had not traveled so far to let her father triumph now.

She tapped O'Reilly on the shoulder and as the older woman turned her head, Celine caught her on the side of the jaw and followed through with all her weight. O'Reilly fell dazed to the ground and could only watch as Celine disappeared into the trees.

Inside the forest Celine looked around. There was no sign of Robert or Jackson and she had no idea which direction they had taken. She chose a direction at random and began to run, vaulting over roots and fallen trees and ignoring the thorns and twigs that tore at her skin. At any moment she expected to hear a scream or the single gunshot that would tell her she was too late. She ran on, breathless, no longer sure of her direction, fearful that she might be traveling in a circle. She stopped and turned around and saw that she had almost missed it: There behind her, twenty yards away, shielded by bushes, was a clearing where the sunlight illuminated a fearful tableau.

Jackson stood up and looked at Robert standing thigh deep in the grave. There was no virtue in any further delay. The girl was not coming to plead for his life. The mission had failed: They were not in love. Now Robert must die, denied that "blissful consummation" as O'Reilly had expressed it, and in doing so he would join the Department. Jackson had heard of killing in the course of missions before, but had always prayed that he would never have to do it himself. Life, he knew, for all its faults was a wonderful thing and to take it away, even in the course of duty, was a terrible burden. He looked around: still no sign of the girl.

"Okay," he said, "I think we've waited long enough."

He tugged the spade from Robert's grasp and threw it aside.

"No," said Robert, falling to his knees and pleading.

"Lie down."

"Please, no."

Jackson pushed Robert facedown into the soft damp earth.

This is how it ends, thought Robert.

Jackson took aim and cocked the gun. "I commit you to His mercy."

The sharp blow on the back of his head caught Jackson just as he pulled the trigger. The bullet thudded into the soil beside Robert's head and he heard the gunshot and the smack of steel against head before Jackson collapsed on top of him. Robert screamed and wriggled free. He looked up to see Celine, spade in hand, staring down at him.

"Come on," she said.

"Who are they?"

"Doesn't matter, just move," she said and reached down to haul him from the pit. Before they left, she prised Jackson's gun from his fingers and stuffed it into her jacket. They fled through the forest to the road, emerging only a short distance from the pickup. Of O'Reilly there was no sign.

They got into the truck and Robert drove.

"Just for a moment," he said, "I thought I was in trouble."

"I told you," Celine said, "keep on going. You shouldn't have stopped. You shouldn't have got out of the car, and you shouldn't have gone into the woods."

"Okay, you were right."

"I'm always right. You might like to remember that."

Robert had a sudden thought. "Have we got the money?"

"Where did you put it?"

"In the back." But just as Celine turned to look, the blade of a knife brushed through the back of Robert's seat missing him narrowly.

Holding the knife was O'Reilly, who on recovering from Celine's punch had a made a swift calculation. Jeopardy, it seemed, had taken effect. The girl had gone to his rescue. If this were so, then the only logical course of action was to place them in still greater danger, to go with the flow. But danger was not something you could simulate; danger had to be real and, unlike Jackson, she had no qualms about getting involved. Hence, when she hid behind the front seat and stuffed her switchblade through, it was with every intention of stabbing Robert. Casualties were an acceptable aspect of war, and what was love, if not war? reasoned O'Reilly, who had taken more from one day of bitter personal experience than all her decades of research.

Robert swerved and O'Reilly rose up behind

him, drawing her gun as she did so. Celine leaped at her and they tussled fiercely. Just as O'Reilly would manage to level the gun at Robert's head, Celine would force it away. Two shots penetrated the roof of the truck and another the windshield. O'Reilly was tough and determined, and Celine found it more and more difficult to resist her. Robert, head down and foot to the floor as the bullets flew past him, screamed at Celine. "Do something!"

Celine thought of Jackson's gun. It lay at her feet but she could not let go of O'Reilly long enough to pick it up. She saw that they were approaching a bridge. There was only one thing for it. She pushed O'Reilly close to one of the doors and reached over to open it. O'Reilly looked down and saw the road running past beneath her in a blur. She knew what was about to happen. She reached for the handle to close the door, but it was too late.

Celine pulled on the hand brake. They went into a skid as they approached the bridge. Robert fought to control the vehicle, but they swung around one hundred and eighty degrees and smashed the truck's side into the parapet.

Celine's last vision of O'Reilly was the look of resignation on her face as she was thrown by the impact out of the vehicle and over the parapet. Too late did Celine realize that in her left hand O'Reilly held the suitcase, and she could only watch helplessly as it followed over the concrete wall and into the abyss.

As O'Reilly fell toward the river some two hundred feet below, she hoped it was all worth it. She and Jackson had done their best. A higher degree of jeopardy was hard to imagine. If true love did not blossom now, then it was not for want of dedication on their parts. With this satisfaction, she prepared to meet the pain that would mark the end of her fall and the beginning of her suffering.

The truck bounced and stopped. Robert and Celine gazed blankly and said nothing for several minutes before opening the doors and stepping down. They stood at the wall and looked beneath them. O'Reilly's body was sprawled inelegantly on a rock in the center of the river, her head and legs at improbable angles. There was no sign of the suitcase, but farther down river, clusters of bank notes could be seen floating away. In a day or two, perhaps longer, they would reach the ocean.

The woman was dead and there was nothing they could do. With the next flood she would be swept from the rock to follow the money down through the gorges and pools until, bloated and discolored and slightly eaten, she would float to the surface near some dock or washed up on a distant shore.

They turned away in silence and returned to the truck, which was scarred but still functioning. Robert turned it around and they continued on their journey across the bridge and beyond without uttering a single word.

If they had continued to watch, they might have seen, an hour or so later, a slight twitching in the fingers of the dead body on the rock. And if they had been foolhardy enough to have clambered down the steep hill to the river and swum across the rapids to the rock, they would have seen that the corpse was breathing, if only slightly, and that her eyes were full of life and pain.

16

When Robert and Celine arrived in the nearest town, about thirty miles on, they had passed through the first stage of shock and were adapting, each in his and her own way, to its residual effects.

Robert, after his initial horror, was relieved to find that the world had not come to an end, that life went on much as before, as it did for example in this town with its stores, fast-food restaurants, motels, and its people going to and fro, interacting and conversing in blissful ignorance of the gruesome death that had occurred only a short distance from their homes. Why, at the gas station they pulled into there was even a Walt-clone to greet them with a hymn to the act of service. A rather poor clone, it must be said, for he spoke his lines without enthusiasm or belief, obviously wishing that the consumer would just go elsewhere and leave him alone with his glossy photographic pleasures.

"Good afternoon," he said, belching, "my name

is, eh—" He paused and Robert relieved him of his misery.

"Don't worry, just fill it up. Please."

Celine was already gone, heading for the retail wing of the facility. As the one who had opened the door and pulled the hand brake, she held herself responsible for O'Reilly's death, and although she knew it was an act of self-preservation, she could not feel happy about it. She sought simply to suppress all thought of the issue, and on arrival at the gas station, she had seen an immediate avenue of diversion. The store was well stocked with cheap electrical goods, toys, and clothes, and before long Celine had amassed an armful of mind-and-body fodder to distract her from the crisis in her soul. A still more potent distraction was already prepared, as she would soon find out.

Outside, while he waited for Walt's unhappy clone to fill the tank, Robert's thoughts had turned to food, a sure sign of recovering composure. He looked along the strip of drive-through houses of food, each with its competitive, all-you-can-eat offers at absurdly low prices, each occupying a niche within a saturated market: Tex-Mex, waffles, shrimps, burgers, noodles, bar-B-Q, and beginning again with Tex-Mex, substituting every third noodles for something called "ranch style." The choice was bewildering, but Robert was not worried: he had been in the U.S. long enough to know that it all tasted the same.

He had settled in his mind for the Waffle House and its pleasingly oval parking lot, where he would order a burger with ranch-style shrimps on the side, but before he could consummate this desire, he knew he must retrieve Celine from her shopping.

As he looked across the forecourt and into the store, he saw that all was not going well. From Celine's wild gesticulations and the firm but obstinate visage of the cashier, he could tell that an argument of some kind was in progress. By the time he had run inside and reached the checkout himself, no words were necessary to explain Celine's distress. Using a large pair of steel scissors, perhaps designed and kept especially for this purpose, the cashier had carefully snipped Celine's credit card into four pieces, which lay on the counter, suddenly transformed from symbol of wealth to worthless plastic.

"Don't worry," said Robert, "I've got cash." From his pocket he produced the last of his limited cash reserve to pay for the gas and some food. They left behind the gadgets, clothes, and toys. Celine stormed away from the store toward the car, snatching the keys from the clone and throwing them to Robert.

"How could he do a thing like that?" she asked as he started the truck and they pulled away.

"Stay calm, okay?" said Robert.

"He canceled my credit card. My own father. How could he do a thing like that? I've never been so humiliated in all my life."

"I know how you feel," said Robert, hoping that empathy might help, but in vain.

"You don't begin to know how I feel," countered Celine, exhibiting for the first time in Robert's presence a full blast of the paternally inherited anger. "Only the exceptionally rich could know how I feel at a moment like this."

"Don't take it personally."

If he had been searching for unhelpful phrases, Robert would have had to work hard to improve on that.

"I'm his daughter—how else am I supposed to take it? What's he trying to say? That I'm going to find my own natural level, sink to the bottom, like her, is that it?"

"Her? Who are you talking about?"

Suddenly Celine became calm. "Pull over," she instructed.

"What for?"

"Just pull over," she repeated in a manner that commanded obedience.

As he drew the vehicle to a halt by the side of the road, Robert followed Celine's gaze to its object and what he saw made his heart sink.

"Oh, no."

Celine was staring at a bank. It stood about fifty yards away, a squat brick building with small windows and a banner stretched above the door advertising FAST LOANS AT LOW RATES. Celine licked her lips. This was the perfect response to everything: to her father, to the credit card, to the death of O'Reilly, and the loss of the money. Furthermore, she reflected with insight, it would be pretty much the high point of a lifelong devotion to bad behavior. She lifted out Jackson's gun from underneath her seat and emptied the food they had bought from its brown paper bag.

"No," said Robert again.

"Live a little," said Celine, checking to see if Jackson's gun was loaded. It was.

"This is dangerous."

"No," said Celine, "back there on the bridge: That was dangerous. This is exciting."

"It's not a good idea."

"Stop worrying, it'll be my first time, too."

"That's what I'm worrying about," said Robert. But Celine was already out of the truck.

"Trust me," she said. "I know what I'm doing."

As they covered the walk and entered the bank, they did not look like armed robbers. Instead they looked like a young couple in a poor financial situation on their way to file an application for a fast loan at low rates, which would undoubtedly turn into a protracted struggle, resulting in a small loan at a crucifying level of interest. Such people were the bank's daily bread and were always welcome, for there were few people so poor that the bank could not screw a profit from them, few people who did not have some form of collateral, be it a truck or a ring or a kidney, that could be put against a loan. So neither Robert's shifty expression and constant fidgeting, nor Celine's icy fatalistic bearing aroused any suspicion from the uniformed security officer at the door, who was, in any case, lost in the fantasies of his trade.

They stood in line behind a plump, flowery

shirted woman and her similarly attired teenage daughter who chewed gum with that unadulterated sullenness that can only be achieved by a self-conscious adolescent who is forced to wear clothes she does not like.

Behind the dense plate glass, two tellers dealt with customers, and behind them a small gang of men and women made phone calls, checked credit ratings, arranged loans, and demanded repayment. The teller at window number three beckoned the mother and daughter forward. Robert and Celine waited at the front of the line. Robert hoped that perhaps this delay would sap Celine's enthusiasm, but there was no sign of it. She was as focused as ever, waiting for her moment to come. The teller, a young woman in a corporate gray suit, summoned them to window number four and Celine did not waste any time.

"I'd like to make a withdrawal," she said, smiling as she showed the teller the gun.

The teller obeyed her training. The glass, she knew, was thick enough to stop the bullet, but she must not antagonize the gunman, or gunwoman in this case. Nor must she hand over the money at the first request. She sat virtually motionless, looking her assailant in the eye while letting her right hand drift slowly outward a few inches toward the touch-sensitive panel that would send an alarm to the nearest center of heavily armed law enforcement.

But Celine was prepared for such a response. Without warning she swung the gun out toward the head of the sullen teenager and thrust the brown bag underneath the glass to the teller. "Fill it."

The occupants of the bank, both employees and

customers, were thrown into a hysterical frenzy. Celine looked the security officer in the eye and he did not dare draw his gun. The mother in the flowery shirt screamed loudly and continued to scream. The teenage daughter froze but did not become more or less sullen. She feared dying, but still more she feared dying in this ridiculous flowery outfit her mother had forced upon her. At least she and mother would part having argued, which is what she had always hoped for.

As the mother screamed and everyone scattered away from the gun, the teller began to fill the bag with bills. Robert watched, aware that he was de facto an armed robber although, without gun, little more than a chaperon to the principal villain.

As the bag filled and Celine kept the gun at the girl's head, her mother turned to plead. "Leave my daughter alone. Please leave her alone."

She went to hold her daughter, but Robert intervened, ushering her away.

"Now don't be stupid," he told her. "Nothing's going to happen."

"She is going to kill my daughter."

"She's not going to kill your daughter."

"Yes, I am," said Celine.

"What?"

"Shut up. Everybody shut up or this girl's brains are going all over the fucking wall! Now hurry up and fill that bag."

The teller increased her rate of filling. The mother sobbed softly.

"Celine—" said Robert.

"Shut up."

"You shouldn't point a gun at girl's head."

This was the moment Celine had been waiting for, the final act of theater. She moved the gun away from the girl, who immediately collapsed gratefully into her mother's arms, and jammed it onto Robert's forehead between his eyes.

"Well," she said, "there was a time you didn't find it so very difficult, did you? In an elevator? Remember?"

And she forced him down onto his knees.

"That was different."

"It didn't feel different to me. It felt like this."

She forced his head back with the barrel of the gun. "Now," she asked him, "do you understand what it felt like? Except that you, unlike me, lacked the balls to pull the trigger."

"Oh God."

"Good-bye, Robert."

He closed his eyes. With so much practice he was becoming quite proficient at preparing to die. His short list of treasured memories was already retrieved from store and immediately available to be played a high speed across his consciousness: childhood, school, family life, first love, happy holidays and the halcyon days when he had cleaned floors for a living. All this shot by in about a nanosecond. Similarly, his final reflections on life and love were still fresh and recycleable, having been used only a couple of hours earlier, so he was able to tell himself that he should have seen this coming, that all the evidence of recent events demonstrated clearly that whenever he thought things couldn't get any worse, they invariably did. It was all over. Such was his economy of thought that he even had room in his brain to formulate some heroic final words.

"Okay," he said, "kill me, but don't touch the girl."

Celine could barely breathe for laughing. As one fit passed, another would follow. Walking was out of the question. Catching her breath in between attacks, she lurched away from the wall of the bank and broke into a stumbling sprint after Robert, who was marching grimly toward the pickup, a bagful of bills in his arms.

He heard her laughter as she caught up with him, but did not turn around. There was nothing to laugh at. No joke that he could see. She was right beside him now.

"Extremely amusing," he said.

" 'Kill me, but don't touch the girl,' " said Celine, mocking his earnest entreaty as she folded into another fit of laughing. "You should have been on television."

"Very funny."

"Oh Robert, what is wrong with you?"

"What's wrong? Crazy bitch, I thought you were going to kill me. That's what's wrong."

Celine stopped laughing.

"Kill you? I wouldn't do that."

"No?"

"No," she said, with a shake of her head.

They had reached the truck. The alarm was sounding in the bank, but they were not listening.

"I'm having a wonderful time," she told him.

"That's good."

"Certainly is."

They kissed with passion and possibly something more, but as they parted and Robert looked toward the bank, he saw that the security guard was standing outside with a gun in his hand. He glanced into the pickup. There, on the backseat plain as day was another Celine, not the one who stood beside him, but one who would be shot in a second from now, one who was dying.

"What's wrong?" asked the one beside him.

He shoved her aside and stood in front, hearing immediately the crack of the gun and feeling the impact of the shot in his leg as he fell to the ground, letting the bag of money fall.

The security guard lowered his gun. From this distance he had not expected to hit anyone—he had only been aiming in the direction of the vehicle. This was the first time he had used his gun in the course of duty and he did not like the feeling. He watched the bills scatter in the wind and the young man writhe in pain as the girl shoved him into the truck. The alarm had sounded and the law would be here soon. He did not try to stop the pickup as the girl drove it away: He had done enough already.

17

Darkness had fallen, but still their journey was not over. Robert lay along the backseat, alternately still, quietly moaning, and then thrashing about in a surge of agony. The pain and the steady loss of blood had taken their toll of his strength. His periods of thrashing were shorter and less vigorous, while more and more he lay passive and inert, muttering to himself. Celine feared that he was becoming delirious. Avoiding the freeways had made their drive long and uncomfortable. They were nearly at their destination and she hoped she had made the right decision. In the back of the car Robert thrashed once more.

"I'm dying, Celine, I think I'm dying. I don't want to die." His voice was weak.

"You're not going to die," Celine told him.

"I don't want to die. Are you taking me to the hospital? I don't want to die in a hospital."

"I'm not taking you to a hospital."

"What!"

Robert sat up, his pain momentarily forgotten as he envisaged Celine taking him to an ancient healer or a psychotherapist.

"What do you mean you're not taking me to a hospital? I demand to go to a hospital. Where are you taking me?"

Celine said nothing. They were almost there, and he would find out soon enough.

The firm metal probe tapped against each of his teeth in turn. Robert squirmed as it sought out a tender upper right molar, and it tapped three times to confirm the finding. "Very nice, very nice indeed," said a confident male voice and the probe was withdrawn.

Elliot sat back. He was enjoying himself for the first time since leaving the hospital. He remembered nothing of his arrival there, carried by paramedics, nor of his first few days after a six-hour operation to remove fragments of bone and bullet from his left frontal lobe. He had gradually become aware of voices speaking to him and a tube in his throat, and after what he later learned was one week, he made a return to full consciousness. The doctors had been surprised by the extent of his recovery. He was very fortunate, they kept telling him, not to have lost his powers of speech or movement, indeed, lucky to have survived at all. Lucky? thought Elliot. Lucky to have been shot in the head? Luck didn't come into it: It was that bitch. They had warned him that friends and family might note personality changes in him, disinhibition, aggression, and so forth, but this didn't worry Elliot since he had no real friends nor any family that he kept in touch with. Furthermore he had always been aggressive and disinhibited: It was just that now he had an excuse.

His only visitor in hospital had been Celine's father, come to smooth things over from a legal standpoint. They got on fine together and Elliot had reassured the old man that there was no question of litigation, criminal or civil. No, Elliot had a far grander, more satisfying plan. Celine had shot him in the head, ruining his career and perhaps his life. Well, he would do the same to her, ruin her life that is, in the only way he knew how: He would marry her. Yes, marry her, and if it drove them both to suicide, then so what? At least he would have revenge.

Naville, however, had been noticeably vague on his daughter's exact whereabouts at the time, and Elliot had returned home in the belief that Celine was being kept in a place of safety. At home he had been bored and restless, thinking constantly of Celine and the serial miseries he would inflict upon her in the course of their doomed marriage. Only in the middle of this night, with Celine's unheralded arrival in the company of the poor, wounded schmuck, had he begun to piece together what had taken place. And when Celine pleaded that he should operate to save the schmuck's life, it was too good an offer to refuse.

With a great display of generosity and professionalism, he had carried Robert through his house to the surgery on the ground floor, where he had laid him gently on the reclining dental chair. He had cleaned the wound and rinsed it with ethanol. It was not too bad: All it needed was a bit of exploration, cleaning out, removal of fabric and bullet, and ligation of a couple of little vessels.

But first of all—old habits die hard and Elliot was one of nature's performers—he had inspected Robert's teeth. And what a sorry sight they were: Only in Britain would an adult be allowed out in public with teeth like that. In America they would be put into quarantine and made the subject of a Senate investigation. They were worse than revolting, they were natural.

"You know," he said to Robert, "you could have a perfect smile."

Robert winced at a burst of pain from his leg. He wished that Elliot would just get on with it.

Celine watched from a chair across the room. She was beginning to think it might have been a mistake to bring Robert here. That Elliot was alive and recovering she had known before her kidnapping, but she had not counted on the pathological exaggeration of his already established personality disorder. He looked crazy, laughing inappropriately, a dressing still taped around his head. The only good thing was that his hand did not seem to shake.

"You could change your smile and your life for two thousand dollars."

"No thanks," said Robert.

"Do you think a perfect smile just happens?" said Elliot a little irritated. "Do you think Celine's smile is her own? No, it's mine. I gave it to her, and I could give you one. For just twelve thousand dollars, I will fix your teeth."

"I didn't get shot in the teeth," Robert said. Elliot laughed.

"Oh, that's funny. You didn't get shot in the teeth. But I'll tell you the truth: It wouldn't have made things any worse if you had." And he laughed again. "If you wait until next year you're going to have to have fifty grand's worth of major reconstruction going on in there."

"If you wait till next year," said Celine who could bear it no more, "he'll be dead."

Elliot scowled. She had spoiled his fun again. Well, just wait. He laid Robert out flat, brought the light down, and searched through his instruments.

"They told me I should take a break. Take a break? Go for counseling? Fuck 'em, they wanted me to stay in the hospital. Discharged myself three days ago. Just as well for you I did, ha?"

He lifted up a scalpel. Robert grabbed his wrist.

"Have you ever done this before?"

Elliot smiled his reassuring you-can-trust-me-I'm-a-dentist smile. "The principles of surgery are the same above and below the neck."

He plunged the scalpel into the edge of the wound, prising it open. Robert screamed.

"Aren't you going to anesthetize me?" he begged, tears in his eyes, practically vomiting.

"Don't worry," said Elliot, "as the pain becomes worse, you'll probably pass out."

Robert awoke in a strange room. Utterly disoriented, it took him several attempts to marshal his thoughts before the picture was complete and he recalled the events of the day and night before. He was lying in a bed, naked but for the bandage around his thigh, in what he presumed was a bedroom in Elliot's home. Early morning light glowed around the edge of the blind. On the wall hung several enlarged photographs of Elliot in various formal and informal situations. In each, his chiseled profile was carefully lit and framed and his range of expression, captured on film, revealed the many sides of the man. In one he might appear at work, dedicated and serious; in another relaxed and friendly as he kneeled beside Latin American children on some vacation beach south of the border; and in yet another, a man at ease with himself and his friends at a poolside cocktail party. And there, in that last one, was a girl on his arm. She was smiling a perfect smile but her eyes were full of sadness.

Robert pulled on his clothes and limped slowly from the room. He found himself in a hallway at the top of a flight of stairs coated in lush green carpet. Around him and lining the stairs were yet more photographs: Elliot skiing, Elliot on a horse, Elliot in London, in Rome, in Africa, swimming through a coral reef, and climbing a mountain. On a landing about halfway down, there was a massive portrait in oils, done in the style of a Dutch master painting James Dean. A small dog lay at Elliot's feet and beside him on a table was a bowl of ripe fruit. Beside this canvas monument and taped to a window so that the daylight might shine through it was the latest addition to the collection. It was a photograph of a sort: a CAT scan of a man's head in cross-section, in which the oval outline of the skull was coarsely punctured at one point and what Robert assumed to be the brain beneath was disrupted and uneven. As he tried to make sense of this, Robert heard voices from a room at the bottom of the stairs. There was the sound of a man laughing deeply, and a woman responded with squeals and giggles. Robert turned from the scan and continued his slow descent.

Inside Elliot's lounge, Celine was involved in a situation that she had foreseen. Elliot's help, she had known, would not come free of charge. His enthusiasm and distorted affability had told her that he expected something in return and it did not take a genius to work out what. The hours that had passed since Robert's ordeal had been exhausting and tedious. At first Elliot had been so excited by his refound surgical prowess that he had talked of little else. He fantasized about retraining in medicine so that he might become a plastic surgeon, pointing out that as Celine aged, he would be able to correct the errors of her flesh, one by one, just as he had punished her dental crimes. All this was innocent enough and she encouraged him to continue, but as the night wore on and he fired up on alcohol and cocaine, his monologue became increasingly carnal and immediate in nature.

He spoke of how he and she would be the most dynamic, most attractive, most beautiful couple who had ever lived, that theirs was a union of perfect beings. Celine had feigned enthusiasm, just as she feigned consumption of alcohol and managed to scatter most of the cocaine. In any case, Elliot was not really watching or listening to her, he was immersed in his own vision and pursuit of satisfaction.

Celine had played a series of flirtatious games, which though they risked exciting Elliot still further, were successful in passing the time. Now they were reaching a critical phase, cavorting seminaked on a rug, passing cherries from mouth to mouth, and it was clear that one or the other must succumb, either she to his charms or he to the complex interaction of alcohol, cocaine, and brain damage. It was at this point that Celine, looking over Elliot's shoulder, saw Robert standing in the doorway, watching with revulsion and disdain. She pushed Elliot away and he turned to see the focus of her attention.

"Robert," he exclaimed as he sprang to his feet, "join the party!" He dropped a cherry into his mouth and spat out the stone before laughing. Robert said nothing, but stared at Celine while she avoided his gaze.

Elliot was delighted. Another chance for the Ubermensch to humiliate the schmuck. He approached Robert with a bottle of champagne and a glass, which he thrust into his hand.

"Drink?" he inquired. "Or something a little stronger?"

"No, thank you," said Robert, still staring at Celine.

"Come on, lighten up a little!" shouted Elliot. He shook the champagne and opened it with ceremony before pouring a frothy load into Robert's glass. "I hear you're something of a fugitive," he continued. "Oh, don't be surprised: Celine and I go back a long way."

"You're her dentist?" said Robert. After Angelo,

he thought, then she began to get trouble with her teeth.

"Yes," said Elliot, "it's true, we met across some bridge work I was doing on that particularly fine set of ivories. I gave her her very first filling."

He sniggered vigorously, and repeated the joke. "First filling. Get it?"

Robert threw the champagne into Elliot's face. Caught by surprise, Elliot blinked and spluttered.

"Now," he said, when he opened his eyes, "I wish you hadn't done that because now I have to hurt you, which is both inconvenient and undignified." He paused. "Nevertheless."

The punch caught Robert square in the center of his abdomen. Handicapped by the pain in his leg, he was unable to do anything but stand there and take it. He fell to the floor, gasping for breath.

"Now stand up!" shouted Elliot.

"Leave him alone," said Celine.

Elliot spun around and pointed at her. His face contorted with fury. "You stay out of this."

Robert was still down on his knees and showed no sign of being about to move. Elliot reached down and pulled him up by his shirt. Robert was aware of pain in his leg and in his stomach, but realized that more was to follow. He let his eyes droop and his head roll back on his limp neck. As Elliot grinned malevolently, Robert sunk his brow with all his force into the top of Elliot's nose. The grip that held Robert's shirt slackened immediately and he watched Elliot slump back onto the floor, blood dripping from his nose. Irresponsible and incorrect as it might be, and despite the hurt that it brought to his forehead, Robert could not deny it: He felt better for that.

They traveled in silence. It had not taken long for them to depart after the fight, but they did not speak until they had left not only the house, but the whole neighborhood. Celine drove, heading no-where in particular, while Robert sat beside her, both of them bristling with self-righteous indigna-tion. They might have gone like this until the pickup ran out of gas, neither one willing to break the deadlock, if a bump in the road had not jarred Rob-ert's leg and provoked an exclamation of pain. Ce-line took this as the beginning of conversation and felt free to fire at will.

"Do you want to explain to me what you were trying to achieve back there?"

But Robert was no fool. He would not be placed on the defensive so early in the conflict. Therefore, instead of answering the question, he selected one aspect of it, more or less at random, and turned it around. He could have said, "Want, since when did you care what I want?" or "Achieve? Why should I have to achieve anything?" But instead it was, "How about you do some explaining to me?"

Inadvertently however, he had handed Celine a ticket to the moral high ground, which she occupied immediately with an almost impregnable motiva-tion.

"I didn't want you to bleed to death and I think I saved your life."

"I would sooner have bled to death than wit-nessed that," retorted Robert, knowing that he had not addressed the issue, but determined to avoid indirect assault on that tricky unassailable high ground.

"Witnessed what exactly?" said Celine, a little carelessly. According to the rules of engagement, she should have remained silent and held on to her advantage.

Robert responded swiftly to this error, seeing immediately an opportunity to portray events in a sordid light. "You and Elliot," said Robert, "in an advanced state of foreplay."

"He was going to pass out drunk in about five minutes if you hadn't come downstairs." Celine was angry to find herself in the role of unconvincing justifier, which Robert had managed to avoid. Even if what she said was true, which it may or may not be, it sounded flimsy and hypothetical.

"Oh sure," said Robert, pressing home his advantage now, but taking care not to leave himself exposed.

Infuriated, Celine spoke now without calculation, "And even if we had been about to engage physically, which we weren't, what's it got to do with you?"

It was a good question. Robert had no reply.

Celine slammed on the brakes and stopped the truck. She looked at him, but he looked away. They had reached it now, the crux of the matter, the consequence of all those things unsaid before, avoided because their plan was to part, but now returning to demand attention.

"You thought we had something?" said Celine.

"It's possible," said Robert quietly.

"But why? Why, Robert? We were getting along

fine, so why do we have to 'have something'? Having something ruins everything."

Robert shrugged.

"So what," continued Celine, "are you going to do now: ask me to marry you?"

Robert responded too quickly. "Of course, I'm not going to ask you to marry me."

"But you'd thought about it?"

"Don't be absurd."

"It never even occurred to you?"

"Wouldn't be so bad," said Robert, who had been thinking about it on and off since the night of the karaoke.

"You see what I mean," said Celine, who had been thinking about it on and off for a similar period. "Just forget it."

"Consider it forgotten," said Robert.

Celine let the engine run. There was nothing more to say on the subject, but the mood was hardly healed. A storm of anger still had to be discharged. Perhaps that anger was with themselves for all their sins of pride and vanity, but neither of the parties was disposed at this moment to such rational thought. It was not long before the anger found its route of dissipation.

"Where do you want to go?" Celine asked, as though there was only one meaning to this.

"I don't care," said Robert with equally false innocence.

"Do you want to get out?"

"Are you asking me to get out?"

"No, I'm asking you if you want to get out."

"That's practically the same thing."

"It's not the same thing at all," said Celine. "One is a request and the other is a question."

"Okay, if that's what you want, I'll get out."

Robert opened the door, inviting reply.

"If that's what you want, I won't stop you."

Robert got out and turned around, holding the door. "Don't even ask where I'm going."

"Don't even imagine that I care," said Celine.

"Exactly the problem," said Robert as he slammed the door shut, glad to have achieved the final word.

Celine put the pickup into gear and drove slowly away. She did not look back as she passed along the tree-lined suburban avenue.

Robert watched the truck disappear over the crest of the hill. Drained of all fury, he felt absolutely nothing. He could not tell whether all this was good or bad, her fault or his, mercy or punishment. He was alone now, that was all he knew for sure, and so he began the long, slow walk, limping painfully toward the last place on earth that might offer comfort to a lonely man.

18

❧

Al was not pleased. He didn't like favors. Favors were messy, difficult to quantify or measure against past or future conduct, favors were trouble all around, but here he was, despite every attempt to discourage it, being asked a favor. It wasn't that he didn't like Robert—no, the kid was nice, decent, honest, polite, not like some kids he could think of. Okay, so he was English, but a man could not be held to account for his parentage. No, what troubled Al was the nature of the situation. Robert had been straight with him, told him the whole story, or most of it, from the day he left the bar to the moment he stomped back in with a bad leg and no money. The kidnapping, the cabin, the ransom, the two bounty hunters, the bank robbery, and the dentist. Al had listened patiently to the whole story, asking for clarification here and there, and at the end of it, he sat and thought while Robert consumed Canadian ham and fries. The kid was in a fix, no doubt about it, a serious fix. Only, why did he have to come here?

"You're the only person I know anymore," said Robert through a mouthful of potato.

"Why don't you go home?"

"Believe me, Al, I would, but I don't have the money for a flight. Come on, just a few weeks, that's all."

"I'd be taking a chance."

"I know. I'm asking you to take a chance."

"I don't want any trouble."

"There won't be any trouble. I don't exist, Al. There's no official record of me. If it makes you happier I'll change my name."

"You done this sort of work before?"

"I worked in a diner before."

"Cooking and cleaning. You don't mind cleaning do you?"

"I've got no problem with cleaning."

Robert watched Al drift away along the bar, lost in his own trenchant analysis of the national malaise.

"I get some young guys: it's cooking, no problem, everybody wants to be the chef, wear the fucking hat, but nobody wants to clean and I tell you that's the whole problem with this country today."

Al paused to think about what he had said. It was true: Nobody wanted to clean. Staff came and went and everything was still covered in dust and grease. Half the time he ended up doing it himself, and him the fucking proprietor. It was a disgrace. But the kid said he could clean: Well, Al would find out soon enough. As for accommodation, Robert could sleep through the back and guard the freezers. Two employees for the price of one.

"Generally, Robert, I don't do favors. But if you don't mind cleaning—"

"Like I say," said Robert, "I've got no problem."

For Celine also, accommodation was an issue to be addressed. As she drove away from Robert, every bit as drained and confused as he, she realized that her options were limited. A return home was out of the question, now or ever: She would never again let her father treat her like some chattel. From now on she would lead her own life, even if it meant poverty, though she hoped it would not.

Poverty, however, was what she faced at present with no money in her wallet and a credit card that had been so cruelly cancelled and dissected. She contemplated a phone call to one or another of her ex-boyfriends, but realized that such an action would more likely end in humiliation than help. Each of those relationships, apart from that with Angelo, had been terminated by her, leaving the suitors hurt and hardly disposed to assist her in her time of need.

Furthermore, Celine knew that many of them had been strengthened by the pain of their doomed liaison with her and once recovered from the initial injury, had gone on to grow in confidence and strength leading successful lives in business and at home, raising families and fortunes as they went. Celine knew of these developments because several of the men in question had taken obvious pleasure in sending her detailed descriptions of their new-found happiness while she wallowed in dysfunctional limbo with Elliot.

Unlikely to find help from these quarters, Celine set out on a journey that took her through places she had never been: past factories and wastelands, vast housing projects, derelict slums, sleazy strips, and burned-out homes. And then, with the last few drops of gas, she pulled off the road and stopped at the edge of a dried-up river. She got out and abandoned the vehicle to the juvenile vultures who would dismantle and recycle it within hours. A well-worn path led down to the riverbed, where she stepped between piles of trash, dead cats, and puddles of oil to reach the other side where the path wound up again. At the top of the bank, she clambered over three giant pipes that carried gas or effluent, and there she saw it, about two hundred yards across the dust, just as she imagined it: the trailer park.

Of course there was another entrance to the park, for vehicles, but Celine had not found that. Instead, by following the path she breached the chicken-wire fence through one of the many man-sized gaps and found herself on the main "street" with rows of trailers standing, end on to her, down either side.

It was a depressing sight. The trailers, painted bright primary colors decades ago, were faded, tattered, and peeling. Stray dogs sniffed along rich trails of scent amongst equally stray children, who played with sticks and bottles. Here and there, a picket fence outlined a plot of dull grass in a poignant attempt at a garden. Ancient automobiles stood beside about half the trailers, serving only to emphasize the place of those in the lowest stratum of American poverty short of the breadline: citizenship without ownership. Celine felt out of place, as indeed she was with her perfect smile and slim physique, in these surroundings without a pool or a butler or a Porsche in sight.

Halfway along the street she found what she was looking for. It didn't seem to have changed much from the photograph she had seen so many years before, sent to her with an inscription in Latin on the back, *"non ignara mali miseris succurrere disco."* "Not unschooled in woe, do I learn to succour unhappiness." Celine noted with relief that this trailer was one of those with a vehicle at its side, a small Ford in two colors where the separate halves had been welded together. It was hardly a symbol of affluence, but a vehicle nevertheless. She picked her way through yet more trash and piles of bottles to the warped door, where she knocked and waited.

Delilah Benich (formerly Naville), had not seen her daughter for eleven years, five months, and three days. In the early days of the separation, then through and after the divorce, she had managed to spend time with the little girl on a regular basis. With a new but promising career in teaching, she had hoped to be able to support both herself and Celine without any dependency on the girl's father, but this was never to happen. Her husband's investigators had provided exaggerated evidence of alcohol abuse and her pursuit of custody had failed. Thereafter her drinking, initially a low-grade response to stress, became a problem in its own right.

Vengeful even beyond the divorce, Naville had used his influence to highlight this problem and she soon found that she had no future in teaching.

From then on, lonely, poor, addicted, and aging, it was downhill all the way, from the rented house to the cheap apartment to the trailer park. For six years now she had lived on handouts and low-paying jobs from which she was invariably fired. Boyfriends came and went, each more useless and parasitic than the last. Robbed of self-esteem and almost constantly drunk, she had failed to meet up with her daughter whenever, in a rare fit of sobriety, she had arranged to do so. Correspondence had become infrequent and then halted altogether, with the final message scrawled on the back of a photograph.

And now, when she opened the door and saw this woman, her daughter, Delilah thought that she was looking at a ghost, the ghost of her younger self. It would not have surprised her if a young Francis Naville had appeared, handsome and attractively ambitious and soon to be corrupted by power and greed. She stood in the doorway, looking at her daughter, looking at the past, and started to cry.

Celine watched the tears roll down her mother's face. She stepped forward and they hugged, both crying now, while the small, stray children watched this strange encounter.

Inside, when they had exhausted their tears on a couch amid the books and bottles, Delilah made them both coffee, lacing her own with bourbon. She passed Celine the cup with a handle.

"And how is that father of yours? Foul piece of shit."

"I haven't seen him recently." Celine stared at her mother, so familiar and so different.

Delilah lit a cigarette. "I'll tell you a story about your father—"

"The dog and the food blender—I already heard it."

Many times she had heard it, between the ages of about six and eight, told her at night before she went to sleep, or rather stayed awake in fear of nightmares. The story may even have been true. Whatever the case, it had passed into the realm of established belief.

"That puppy did nothing to hurt your father. He had no cause whatsoever—"

"Mother," Celine interrupted, "I have something to tell you."

"On our wedding night—"

"He wore his socks in bed. I know."

"He wore his socks in bed with another woman. I tell you, my girl, your conception was practically a miracle. Lying, cheating son-of-a-bitch, I hope he rots in hell."

Celine took a deep breath and broke in, "I killed someone. A woman."

Her mother blew smoke rings. "These things happen."

"Is that all you can say?"

"Maybe it was an accident."

"It was deliberate. I shoved her out of a car."

"Why?"

"It's complicated. She had a gun and—"

"Stop. It's self-defense. You don't need to say another word, not one single word. She pulled a gun, you defended yourself. *Quod erat demonstrandum.* If she was alive, you'd be suing for assault. Now why don't you tell me about this guy?"

"What guy?" said Celine, caught off guard.

"This guy you're not telling me about, that's who."

Delilah put down her drink. This, she knew, was why she should have been there for all those years when her little girl was growing up. She looked at her daughter with pride and affection.

"A mother knows, Celine, a mother knows."

19

Rescued O'R. Badly hurt. Expense likely.
Hope success.

Jackson's entry in his diary for late October was
accurate but hardly complete. He had lain unconscious in the forest grave until nightfall, then stumbled blindly through the wood, calling in vain for
O'Reilly until daylight came and he found the road.
Reaching the bridge, he had noticed the tire tracks
at the point of the accident and, looking over the
parapet, he was shocked to see O'Reilly so far
below, still flaccid and bent across the rock.

She was very badly injured. At the local hospital,
it was all that Jackson could do to prevent them
from pronouncing her dead on arrival when he laid
her cold, damaged body on the stretcher. Her body
temperature was not compatible with life, they explained; she was too far gone to rewarm. In addition, they catalogued her fractures—of skull, spine,
pelvis, both hips, several ribs, and a crush injury to

her right arm. The damage to her vital organs was equally extensive and there was no pulse, respiration, or cardiographic activity.

"She's dead," they told him.

"She can't die," said Jackson. "She's just cold."

They took him to an office where a doctor sat down with him and explained it all again. Meanwhile they shipped O'Reilly to the mortuary. The mortuary was cold, but not as cold as where O'Reilly had spent the night, and before long the attendants were horrified to hear a knocking from inside the cabinet. It was O'Reilly, swinging her left arm against the metal partition.

"I told you," said Jackson, "she can't die."

They wrapped her in aluminum-foil blankets and filled her full of warm fluid. She was transferred by helicopter to a major teaching hospital, where they took one look at her in the ICU and told Jackson, "She's going to die."

"No," said Jackson, "she can't die. She just needs your help to get well quicker."

A series of operations followed. At each, the surgeons were surprised to find that the patient was indeed still alive, given the extent of her injuries. Grave prognoses were given, but with less and less confidence each day, for as they stitched and stapled her back together, she began to heal almost before their eyes.

And the brain damage, the irreversible, terminal, incompatible-with-life brain damage that they had all been pinning their reputations on, well, that never amounted to very much more than a headache during her first days of consciousness.

"We thought you were going to die," they told her.

"I can't," she told them but looked less than happy about it, as though recovery were a disappointment.

Then came the day, barely a month after her admission, when she was ready for discharge. She was able to walk, only short distances to begin with but increasing rapidly. She had all her faculties and the only outward sign of her multiple trauma was a right arm still encased in plaster. A remarkable recovery.

All that remained was payment.

Naville was waiting for them in a corridor outside the hospital finance office. Inside, he had signed a check for a substantial sum and had cursed himself for agreeing to meet medical costs. Too soft, he thought, I'm too soft. Even with her rapid recovery, the cost of O'Reilly's care was outrageous. Naville had never realized that health care could generate so much profit and he resolved to buy heavily into it.

"We're very grateful, Mr. Naville," said Jackson.

"According to the doctor, you should have been dead," Naville told O'Reilly. "In fact, from my point of view it would have been a lot cheaper."

"Like my partner says, we're grateful."

"And he's still out there."

"We know."

"And he's got my money."

Jackson and O'Reilly avoided his eye. They had neglected to tell him about the money, feeling that there was only so much bad news a man could take.

"And my daughter: Where is she? Alive? Dead? We don't know."

Again they avoided his eye. They knew perfectly well where she was. Men and women are predictable creatures and it had not taken Jackson long to find both Robert and Celine.

"Look, Mr. Naville," he said, "suppose we find your daughter, alive and well. Okay, and this guy—he's no threat to you. Why waste your time? Write off the money as a bad debt. What's the point in revenge?"

"I might say the point was the bullet in my leg," hissed Naville, "or all the upset and the aggravation, but it's not. It's the principle. Do you understand that? Or do I have to find someone who does?"

"We understand," said O'Reilly. "My advice to you, sir, is to go home, relax, and wait for the phone to ring."

But Naville did not relax. To do so would have broken the habit of a lifetime. Not that he didn't try, but golf, aromatherapy, transcendental meditation, and cannabis had all failed, mainly because he didn't like being relaxed. Far more did he enjoy being fired up and aggressive: That was his natural state. Only when the stress of his anger became unbearable for his muscles and skeleton and they cried out for mercy would he submit to a soothing, but not particularly relaxing, massage from the deft, brutal hands of Mayhew.

And so later that day, having bought heavily into health care and so recouped some of the money he had paid out earlier, Naville lay naked, facedown on a marble slab in the steam room beneath his mansion. On one side, Mayhew, also naked, hunched over Naville's back, sweating as he kneaded, smacked, stretched, and pressed the tense flesh of his employer.

Mayhew had been going through a process of personal reevaluation. The dismay he had felt at watching Jackson and O'Reilly had told him that in the fashion of a leopard, he could not change his spots. Buddhism, he realized with a mixture of sadness and relief, was nothing more than a passing phase in his life, a short experiment that had defined his boundaries as a person rather than extended them.

It was to be expected. Twenty-five years he had spent as one of Her Majesty's finest killing machines, sent to kill or be killed wherever her ministers felt appropriate, without question or hesitation. And then twenty more years serving masters perhaps less respectable than her, but often more generous.

Most of that latter period had been in the employ of Mr. Naville, and very satisfactory it had been: a little spot of rough stuff near the beginning, with a role in service more suited to his years thereafter. He had run the affairs of the house with the same precision that he had stormed jumbo jets on distant runways and ambushed freedom fighters on jungle trails. He had watched Celine grow up with amazement, for as an only child himself with no family of his own, a little girl was considerable novelty. He had punished her kidnappers and taught her to shoot, played her games and watched the series of young men come to founder on the rocks of her temperament.

Never, though, had he considered her as a woman. Such thoughts were not his habit. He had preferred a solitary life, unhindered by emotional ties, and even within the loner-filled ranks of the world's elite divisions, he had stood out as a man with no friends of either sex. But despite denying himself all emotional or sexual attraction, he was still offended by Celine's kidnap. It suggested a slackness on his part, even though he was not present at its occurrence.

Then to watch Naville hire Jackson and O'Reilly and to listen to their excuses, it was all too much. He had kissed his effigy of Buddha for the last time, placed it in a box, and locked it in a cabinet along with his robes, carefully folded, and his candles. From another cabinet he lifted a similar box, but inside this was no token of peace. It had been ten years since he last put a man to sleep forever, but Mayhew was as ready and willing now as he had ever been. All that remained was to persuade Naville.

"You are very tense, sir. Try to relax. I'm sure they'll manage to bring Miss Celine back in one piece, or possibly two." He ground his fist into the small of Naville's back, causing him to squirm.

"All right," said Naville, "if you're so smart, let's hear it."

"I am merely suggesting, sir, that rather than continuing to place your trust in the two feckless bozos"—he brought the flat of his hand down hard on Naville's neck—"you might consider an alternative."

"I don't know. Might just make things worse."

Mayhew took his employer's right arm and stretched it out. Then, placing one arm in Naville's armpit to anchor himself, Mayhew prepared to give a violent pull. "In the Royal Marines, sir, we observed an old military dictum: Never Reinforce Failure."

Naville screamed, but no one could hear.

In Jackson and O'Reilly's apartment the walls were covered in photographs of Robert and Celine. Taken through telephoto lenses, they were often blurred and not particularly exciting: Robert cleaning, Robert serving, Robert cleaning again, or Celine sitting in her mother's trailer, reading a book. There was no sign of progress. They were leading separate lives and neither showed the slightest sign of being about to look for the other.

For Jackson and O'Reilly, this was a problem. Their money was running out, as was Naville's patience. The discomforts of actually living were as sharply felt as ever, even by O'Reilly, who had previously maintained an unaffected air.

In this atmosphere of desperation they had concocted a plan using methods that neither had ever employed before. O'Reilly, assessing her partner as the more creative half of the team, had awarded to him the responsibility of setting this plan in motion. But while Jackson sat at the table, a pen in his hand and a piece of paper lying blank before him, she could not resist the urge to interfere, and prowled back and forth behind him, peering impatiently over his shoulder.

"Stop hovering over me," said Jackson, "I can't concentrate."

"Have you written anything yet?"

"What am I supposed to write?"

"Love letters, Jackson, deal mainly with the subject of love."

O'Reilly based this opinion solely on her extensive research, for never in the short course of her own tragic romance did she receive or send such a letter.

"I need time to think."

"We don't have time. Every day they spend apart, the more difficult it's going to be. And if Naville finds our boy, he's just meat. So think, Jackson, have you ever done this before?"

Jackson did not have to search far in his memory. She had a pretty face and when she laughed, which was often, her eyes would sparkle.

"Well, back when I was alive, there was a girl."

He had helped her to cross a river in flood. They met again in town. They did not care what people thought.

"You never told me about this," said O'Reilly.

"It never came to nothing, O'Reilly. Her father did not approve our match. It was just young love. But I wrote many times, with passion and despair."

All true. Her father had objected, placed obstacles in Jackson's path, but still they were not discouraged and many were the stumbling, heartfelt words that reached her through servants or were left in hollow trunks of dead trees.

"I never knew you had a romantic soul." O'Reilly was touched by this display and she envied such a well of emotion.

"I often wonder what became of that girl: sweet Eliza. Eliza Gray." He smiled at the picture in his mind, but his face soon clouded over as another memory forced its way through. A moonless night in Alabama. A young man out walking underneath the stars, returning from some hurried rendezvous, an exchange of keepsakes and tender words, of promises and a kiss. Harsh voices interrupt his stride.

"That looks like a black boy to me."

"What's a black boy doing out at this time?"

"Where you been, nigger?"

The dogs bite and a rope loops over the bough of a tree. It is three days before anyone has the courage to cut down the body. That blissful consummation, O'Reilly had called it, the communion of souls, denied to them.

"Her father was a colonel."

"Jackson," said O'Reilly, "I know it hurts, but you're qualified. You can write this letter."

"Well, that's the problem. I wrote to her, sure, but I didn't write letters."

"What then?"

"Well, as a matter of fact," said Jackson, "I wrote love poems."

Mail was rarely delivered to the trailer park. Most who lived there had long since rejected or been rejected by all who might correspond with them and the ship of welfare had long since sailed on, leaving them to sink or swim alone in its wake. Demands for payment for one thing or another, fines, or loan-default notices were the only regular deliveries, and not in living memory had such a fragrant, clean, and personal-looking envelope been seen as that which was placed a few days later in the mailbox of Delilah Benich (formerly Naville).

Delilah held it to the light and considered steaming it open, (another aspect of motherhood that she felt she had missed), but it would not reveal its secrets. Instead she handed it to her daughter with a word to the wise.

"Remember, my dear, they only want one thing. Maybe they want it more than once, but it's still only one thing."

Celine tore open the envelope and removed the single sheet of white paper enclosed. She read, then read again. Then at night she folded the sheet of paper and placed it under her pillow. And though her mother begged her as only a mother can, Celine would not declare its origin or content.

20

The rain fell heavily on Jackson and O'Reilly. Seven days had elapsed since the night of Jackson's composition and for the last three they had spent all evening on this rooftop directly across the street from Al's Bar. From here, with their binoculars they had watched all the comings and goings from the bar, but there had been no sign of Celine. They were worried: Perhaps the letter had not been delivered, perhaps her mother had intercepted it, perhaps Jackson had written Robert's address incorrectly. All of these were possible, but most probably, they feared, she was simply not coming because she did not want to.

With the aid of eavesdropping equipment, installed inside the bar by O'Reilly one afternoon when Robert was not there, they were able to listen to the conversations between Al and Robert when the bar had closed. They talked mainly about cleaning floors and the reluctance of young people to become involved in same. Robert did not mention

Celine once. Worse still, it emerged that he was saving money to pay for a flight home to Scotland—thousands of miles away. Once that happened, it would be all over, and Jackson and O'Reilly could settle down to an infinite stretch of earthly misery.

There was no sign of her. O'Reilly was becoming irritable, annoyed with herself as much as anything for a) pursuing such a hopeless scheme, and b) trusting Jackson to perform such a pivotal role within it.

"I wish you'd let me read that poem," she said.

"A poem is a very personal document," said Jackson, who knew about such things.

"I hope it was a good one, Jackson, that's all I'm saying, because if she don't like it, she won't come. And if she don't come: We're stuck."

Jackson did not reply. He was disheartened. He had put so much into the poem, so much raw emotion, that he could not believe she would not respond, and yet she had not come. It was enough to damage his faith both in human nature and in his own prowess as a poet. How could anyone be so hard? He watched as the last drinkers and diners left Al's Bar and the red neon sign was switched off. Soon, as on the other nights, Robert would finish cleaning and then retire to the back room, while Al, when he had finished counting the money, would wish Robert good night and lock the doors as he left.

The rain continued to fall.

"I should have read it," said O'Reilly. "I should have wrote it. I can't believe I let you do it. William fucking Shakespeare."

Jackson gasped. A car had pulled up outside the

bar. An old Ford, two colors where it had been welded together. He scrambled for his binoculars.

"I knew she'd come."

They watched as Celine dashed through the rain
from the Ford to the doorway of the bar.

Inside, it was the end of another long, but
profitable evening. Al calculated the day's takings
while Robert swished the mop rhythmically back
and forth across the floor studded with cigarettes,
nuts, grease, glass, and pools of beer. He still
walked with a slight limp, but his injury was healing, just as his recall of Celine was fading. He had
put all that behind him: Now his thoughts were on
home and how to get there.

He heard the door of the bar swing open and
close again. He turned around just as Al told Celine,
"Sorry, lady, we're closed now."

But Celine ignored him. She stood a few feet in
from the door, staring at Robert. Al looked at them
both. So this was the one, he thought, the kidnapped girl that Robert had told him about. He
sensed that his presence was not required.

"I'm just going to check some stock," he said as
he retreated through the door, pausing to take a
final look at Celine. Nice-looking woman, he
thought.

"I got your poem," Celine said.

"Sorry?" Robert said, relieved that there seemed
to be some purpose to this meeting.

"Your poem. The one you sent me."

"Poem?"

Celine pulled the envelope from inside her coat
and lifted out the sheet of white paper.

* * *

Up on the rooftop Jackson watched through the binoculars, his heart racing, while O'Reilly adjusted the volume on their electronic receiver. This was their final chance. They listened to Celine's soft voice as she began to recite the poem.

> "Oh desert me, wretched loneliness,
> And bring me back my love.
> For she and I have parted
> And the sky is up above."

Jackson was ecstatic. Just by the tone of her voice he could tell. "It's worked. She loves it."

And why not, he thought. It was good. It rhymed, it scanned, it subtly evoked all sorts of stuff, like wretched loneliness and love and parting and the sky being up above, all kind of multilayered and self-explanatory at the same time. O'Reilly was less convinced.

" 'Sky up above'? What the fuck is that about?"

"It means the world goes on, even though they've parted and are wretchedly lonely. It's a conventional poetic technique to contrast the universe with the inner world."

"Sounded to me like it was just there to rhyme."

"Shh."

Celine had started on her second verse.

"Your limbs so svelte and slender, / Your touch so soft and tender, / But the bit that I like best . . . And I'm not going to read that line."

"Jackson, what the hell did you write?"

"Just a simple poetic reference to her, you know . . ."

"Breasts?"

"Breast."

"Singular?"

"Yes. The plural wouldn't rhyme properly."

"Jesus, Jackson!"

"Poetry can deal legitimately with the physical as well as the emotional, you know. A lot of classic poetry is extremely graphic, if you read it carefully."

"We're lucky she didn't call a lawyer."

"Celine," they heard Robert's voice, "I don't know why—"

"The last verse, Robert."

On the rooftop they listened again.

> "Just as the flower blossoms
>   In the gaze of the shining sun,
>   I would be most honored
>   If you would bear my son."

O'Reilly struck Jackson a sharp blow to the head with the parabolic microphone and kicked him in the shin. She followed up by swinging her right arm, still in plaster, into his belly.

"You dumb male chauvinist asshole. What is she going to think? She got a poem from a stalker, that's what. Jackson, this is the nineteen-nineties and you wrote an ode to fertility. She's a woman, not a test tube."

Jackson raised his arms to protect himself from the torrent of blows that O'Reilly rained upon him, while down in the bar Celine continued.

"Robert, no one ever wrote me a poem before. Most of the guys I dated, like Elliot, they didn't care about me, they just wanted to own me."

O'Reilly, about to poke her partner in both eyes, drew back. Unable to believe that she was hearing, she turned the volume up full on her earpiece. This was it, at last: It had happened, they could hear it happening.

"I would never open myself up to any of those guys, but until I met you I never believed there was any alternative. When you stopped that bullet and then you got the wrong idea about Elliot, I should have understood. And when we argued and you got out and I drove away, I should have realized that you can only fight like that when there's something special to fight about."

"Celine." It was Robert's voice.

"Let me finish. This is difficult for me to say, but I feel I can trust you, and I—"

"Celine—I didn't write that poem."

"You what?"

"I didn't write it. I never wrote a poem in my life."

On the rooftop the jubilation, so short lived, had turned again to horror and dismay.

"What is he doing?" said Jackson. "Oh, God, no."

"How can anyone be that honest?"

O'Reilly peered through the binoculars, hoping with every atom of her soul to send a message.

"It's his handwriting. Tell him it's his hand-writing."

"But it's your handwriting," said Celine. "It's got your address on it. It's even got some sort of cheap aftershave impregnated into the paper."

"I didn't write it."

"Oh, God," said O'Reilly. She fell to her knees

and tore off the headset just as Celine emerged from the bar, running through the rain to her car. O'Reilly felt Jackson place an arm around her and she drew close to him. It wasn't fair. They had tried so hard, suffered so much, and come so close, but still they had failed in their mission. Success, against all the odds, had been only words away. They could have been away from here in minutes, back where they belonged, instead of returning to some roach-infested apartment for stale food and uncomfortable sleep. But now that was all they had to look forward to forever, just because this mismatched and inappropriate couple had failed to see each other's charms.

O'Reilly thought back to her own life. No one had given her such chances, no one had worked so hard to bring her love and happiness. She would have settled for just a fraction of what they done for Robert and Celine. Instead, her life had been desolate and empty at the end, victim to the forces of random unhappiness.

"Mortal fucking beings, what do you have to do?"

"I'm sorry," said Jackson, as he held her in the shelter of his body.

"It's not your fault. At least you tried."

Jackson could feel her shake as her tears began to flow. He felt helpless and this made him angry. Many things he could endure, but this was too much. Cold, heat, indigestion, constipation, toothache, chest pain, all these he would complain about, but they would not deflect him from his purpose. Poverty, sleeplessness, being hit with a shovel, even failure in the mission, to all these he would grow accustomed, but O'Reilly being upset, that he could never tolerate.

In all the time they had worked together, there had never been much exchange of emotion. For the first decade they had hardly exchanged a word, and conversation since had been principally argument. But each had come to respect the other's strengths and to regard their weaknesses as endearing. For Jackson, to work with anyone else would be unthinkable. He depended on her aggression as surely as she did his philosophical introspection. But now she was upset. He let out his fury.

"It didn't work! It didn't work. Those bastards! Those selfish little bastards. We did everything for them: brought them together, put them in jeopardy, damn near killed them both. All they had to do was fall in love and we could have gone home. But would they? Would they? Oh no, not those selfish little bastards."

Alone in the bar, Robert found to his surprise that he still held the mop in his hand. How appropriate, he thought: Cleaning floors was what he wanted to do when she had entered his life, and cleaning a floor was what he did as she left it. He had blown it, he knew, but perhaps it was better that way. He could think of excuses, but they couldn't disguise the fact. He could cite his surprise, his confusion, the handwriting (just like his), but still he had blown it.

He had meant to say so much more than just "I didn't write it." He had meant to tell her that he was glad to see her, that she looked great, that he missed her company, but he had realized in retrospect that they were too different as people to go any further. She was right, he believed—having something would ruin everything, and they had come perilously close to having something. Better to keep it casual. That way they could be friends in the future. All this he had meant to say, but he realized he had blown it. In his haste to dissociate himself from the juvenile doggerel, he had seemed to reject her. It wasn't what he meant to do, but maybe it was better that way. Yes, he told himself firmly, it was all for the best.

The old Ford would not start. The heavy rain had seeped through gaps in the rusting bodywork and trickled into all corners of the engine where water should not be. Celine twisted the key in the ignition repeatedly, but though the motor turned over, it would not kick into life.

Celine paused, thinking perhaps she had flooded the engine, and twisted instead a knife of loathing into her own heart. Loathing for herself first of all. What a fool she must have looked, wandering into the bar and reciting that dumb poem. She looked at it once again before she tore it up. What a piece of crap. No wonder he disowned it. She couldn't understand why it had moved her so much in the first place. Okay, so no one had ever written her a poem before, and when she got it, she realized how much she liked him and how different he was from all those other jerks, but that was obviously a big mistake. "I would be most grateful if you would bear my son." Who did he think he was?

And she transferred some loathing to Robert. What a fool he was, treating her like that. He'd be sorry. She had a life ahead of her, but what was he? Nothing. Nobody. A cleaner.

Done with loathing for the moment, she turned the key again, but still the car would not start. Rather than loathe again, she switched on the radio. It took her two or three bars to realize what song it was: a popular classic, a celebration of the durability and strength of love, it told of one who has, through his own folly, lost his lover, but finds himself unable to forget and tormented by regret. Celine did not want to hear this song.

She pressed "Off" but it kept on playing, rising up to the point where the singer castigates himself for not setting aside enough quality time for the relationship.

She pressed "Off" again, but the switch was broken. Similarly, the volume would not go down. If anything, it was getting louder. Just as the singer began to reprise the whole theme, she brought her foot up and, using the heel of her shoe, she smashed the face of the radio. It fell silent at last. She hoped her mother would understand.

From the rooftop, O'Reilly observed Celine's efforts to start the car. The tears had stopped now and the calm, rational O'Reilly had taken charge again. The mission was finished, that much was clear. So they had to move on, to make themselves as comfortable as possible on this earth as they stared into infinity. As she looked at Celine, a plan formed in her mind, attractively simple, direct and immediate.

"Maybe we've failed, Jackson, but we don't have to live like this."

Jackson, packing away the equipment, was morose beyond consolation. "How come?"

"Have you ever kidnapped anyone?"

"Man or a woman?"

"For God's sake, Jackson: either."

"No."

"Then it'll be the first time for both of us."

They looked down. Drifting up from the road, muffled by the damp air, came the faltering whine of an engine that would not start. At least the laws of mechanics were on their side.

Al, having checked the stock out back for as long a time as he thought was polite, returned to the bar. He was not surprised to find Robert alone, mop in hand.

"She gone?" he asked.

"Yes," said Robert.

"Nice-looking woman."

"She's not my type."

This was too much for Al. Sooner or later the kid was going to have to get a grip on reality. Kidnapping, bank raids, what kind of life was that for a young man? No wonder he couldn't think straight. For example: She's not my type.

"What are you talking about?" Al said. "Look at yourself. You're nobody. You're nothing. You're wanted in connection with a violent crime. You're cleaning the floor of a diner. She is an intelligent, passionate, beautiful, rich woman. The issue of whether or not she is 'your type' is not one that you are likely to have to resolve in this world or, indeed, the next, since she will be going to some heaven for glamorous pussy and you will be cleaning the floor of a diner in hell."

"I guess so," said Robert. He couldn't argue. As an objective analysis of his situation it couldn't be faulted.

"So why are you even thinking about it?"

"I don't know."

It was true, he didn't know. Why was he even thinking about it? He had no reason, unless Al was wrong, unless it was an issue that he would have to resolve. And if Al was wrong, then perhaps he was wrong himself. He thought back to the day when he had kidnapped her, to the way he felt when he thought she had escaped, the intoxicated insanity of their first night together and the relaxed pleasures of the days that had followed. Suddenly he realized that having something did not ruin everything, it *was* everything.

He dropped the mop and ran to the door. It was the car that he recognized first: the Oldsmobile. It still had the bullet hole in the side where one of his shots had hit. It was pulled up alongside the Ford and a man was trying to drag Celine out of that and into the back of the other car.

In the yellow glow of the streetlight, Robert recognized the man, and then the woman at the wheel of the Oldsmobile. He couldn't believe it: She should have been dead, she must have been dead, they'd seen her corpse lying broken on the rock. She had no right to be alive.

In shock he watched Jackson prise Celine's fingers from the steering wheel and bundle her into the back. When she struggled there, he produced a can of mace and sprayed her face as the woman hit the accelerator and the car raced away.

So far as Al could make out, Robert wasn't talking any sense at all. For half an hour he had listened to him talking about how the woman must be a ghost and that the man might also be one, and that these two ghosts had kidnapped the girl. Al could see all sorts of flaws in this. One: Robert had not actually inspected the body, so the woman might have been merely stunned by the two hundred foot fall onto the rock. Two: Ghosts did not exist. Three: If they did exist, it was not within the realm of conventional ghost behavior to drive an Oldsmobile and kidnap pretty girls. No, he pointed out, if (and it was only if) the woman were a ghost, then she would be pretty much obliged to haunt the scene of her death, i.e., the bridge, and confine herself to poltergeist activity in that locale.

Robert could see the reason in this.

Far more likely, Al continued, the man and the woman were either not the same ones, just similar, or, more likely, they were the same ones, and Robert had overestimated the extent of her injuries. That would explain her appearance of being alive, (because she was), and the kidnapping of Celine (revenge). All that remained was for Robert to rescue her, although how that was supposed to happen, neither had any idea.

Al laid out the options.

"It's a difficult one, Robert. Maybe you'll find resources you never knew you had. On the other hand, maybe not. Maybe she'll die a slow, miserable death at the hands of these two felons and you'll feel guilty for the rest of your life."

"Thanks, Al."

"Just telling you straight, Robert."

"So what am I going to do?"

"Depends on what you want: a lifetime of regret or the woman of your dreams."

Al, having reached the stage of presenting Robert with a choice, was pleased to produce the polished mahogany box from under the bar. It flipped open. Inside, the blade glowed with energy.

Robert was drawn toward it. It was the ease way out. The knife would tell him what to do, remove from him all the responsibilities of choice. But something that Al had said prevented Robert from lifting the knife.

"The woman of your dreams."

Robert knew that for such a woman he must act of his own free will. He viewed the knife as the way of a coward.

"No thanks, Al, tonight, I make my own decision."

Al was a little hurt. "So how are you going to find them? I mean, guys like that, they don't exactly leave a calling card, do they?"

Robert put a hand in his pocket and pulled out his wallet. Inside that, creased and dog-eared, was a memento from the day that his life had changed. It was a business card with an address, above which was printed the title FIRM BUT FAIR COLLECTION AND EVICTION AGENCY.

* * *

Outside the rain continued to fall. Standing in the shadows, a strong, upright man of military bearing waited to see what would happen next. His raincoat was soaked through, water ran down his back and his feet were freezing, but Mayhew did not care. Such discomforts were pleasure to him, for they recalled days gone by, spent on lengthy surveillance or hiding up to his neck in a swamp with the last of his ammunition secreted internally. Those were the days. Killing days.

He had followed Jackson and O'Reilly, anticipating that they would lead him to Robert and Celine. He had planned to kill Robert, retrieve the money, and return Celine to her father, but finding the situation more complex than was expected, he had watched the pantomime unfold with interest. There was, he thought, more fun to be had out of all this. A plan hatched in his mind, a plan that would deal with all issues and problems at once, leaving no loose ends nor waggling tongues.

21

*"T*hank you. No message. I'll call later."

O'Reilly replaced the receiver. "Your father's not at work yet. Boy, is he going to get a surprise."

A few feet away in the lounge of the cramped apartment, Celine sat at a small table. She was tied to a wooden chair and thick tape had been strapped across her mouth. A tennis sweatband was stretched over her forehead.

Jackson was seated across the table from her, his jacket off and his sleeves rolled up. He hadn't been so happy for a long time. The kidnapping of Celine had filled him with pleasure, for at last they were acting in their own interests, masters of their own destiny, instead of having to worry about everyone else's.

The prospect of wealth had proved excellent compensation for the horrors of eternal life; indeed, it almost made it seem worthwhile. His imagination had run riot in considering the sheer number of zeros that might be tagged onto their ransom demand, for he knew that Naville was a wealthy man. Already he had set aside vast hypothetical sums into accounts labeled LEISURE, REAL ESTATE, FIRST-CLASS MEDICAL CARE, and PRIVATE HELICOPTER. His long-term plan, after spending a few decades hopping from one tropical paradise to another, was to buy a farm somewhere in the northwest and raise hogs, although his would be a paternalistic, managerial role rather than an actual hog-handling one. Perhaps in time he would set up a charitable foundation or a scholarship bearing his name. As a diverting side project, he would hunt down the descendants of the men who had murdered him and then convey upon them the gift of forgiveness. His generosity would be legend, but he would not erode his capital base.

Although he anticipated much immeasurable wealth in the next few days, he had seen an opportunity to make a quick buck even sooner. Celine, he reasoned, must be worth some fraction of her father, and here she was, captive in their midst, with nothing to do while they awaited their loot. What better way to pass the time than a session of blackjack. Her condition, gagged and bound, did not present any obstacle: It simply meant that Jackson would need to interpret her wishes as best he could.

Strange to report, his interpretation was that Celine wished to make a series of rash bets on hopeless hands and to take too many hits when she had already won, so that she invariably went bust.

Unable to challenge this policy, Celine had watched helplessly while her losses mounted.

Two tens lay before her.

"You want a hit?" asked Jackson.

She shook her head.

"You sure?"

She shook her head again.

"Okay. It's up to you." Jackson turned over a five.

"Aw, gee. Bust again. Okay, that's another four hundred dollars, so you owe me now three thousand, three hundred and fifty. We'll waive the cents. I take it you're good for your debts."

He made a note of his win, shuffled the cards and prepared to deal again.

Celine closed her eyes. She was exhausted. On recovering from the mace attack, she had rationalized, as Al had, O'Reilly's remarkable powers of survival and recovery. Being kidnapped was not in itself a source of great distress to her, being something of a veteran, but at this particular time, with such chaos in her personal life, it was an unwelcome complication.

It served her father right, of course, for hiring such cut-rate thugs, but she wished they had chosen some other way of robbing him. All she wanted to do now was sleep, but all night Jackson had insisted on this futile, one-sided card game. He had started with stakes of ten or twenty cents, but as his certainty of victory and open cheating increased, so had the scale of his bets. For all Celine cared, he could bet in millions, it would make no difference: She didn't have a dime.

O'Reilly looked at the young woman and thought she ought to make Jackson let her sleep. But, in keeping with her normal, thorough approach, she had researched the theory and practice of kidnapping with a session of skim-reading during the night, and from this she knew that kindness and humanity would not be rewarded. Unrelenting cruelty was the order of the day and depriving the victim of sleep was one aspect of that. It seemed a bit tough, but there it was in all the authoritative texts: Deprive the victim of sleep.

"I don't expect he'll pay our ransom straight off," she told Celine, while Jackson shuffled the deck, "not until we send a few of your fingers through the mail."

Celine gave O'Reilly a look that said she was not convinced by this.

"You see, Miss Naville," continued O'Reilly, "it is your misfortune to have become a commodity, and as a commodity you may be bought and sold according to the demands of the market. Your father may not like that, but I'm sure he'll understand. After all, he's a firm believer in the virtues of unregulated capitalism."

Capitalism was much on O'Reilly's mind at this time, for as well as researching basic kidnapping, theory and practice, she had, like Jackson, mentally assigned her share of the takings. Not for her, though, the pleasures of raising hogs. She had read enough about the great junk bondsmen of the eighties to know that her future lay on Wall Street, as mistress of the universe.

Jackson dealt. He looked at his own cards: nine and seven.

"Okay, I'm happy with sixteen. What about you?" He turned Celine's cards over: four and six.

"Nice cards. Let's say you feel confident. You want to bet, say, four thousand dollars."

Celine shrugged.

"Now, you want a hit?"

He turned over a card. Another four. "Another hit?"

He turned the next card. Three. Jackson frowned and turned the next. Another three. Damn, he thought: twenty. Celine was agitated now, struggling to vocalize through the tape.

"You want another hit?"

Celine shook her head frantically. She had sensed the opportunity to score some small victory over her captors and would not let it pass.

"Are you sure? You already have a five-card trick. You could stick there and you've won four thousand dollars. But if you want another hit—"

Jackson flexed his fingers and prepared to turn the top card on the deck. He knew it would not be an ace, for he had taken the precaution of removing all the aces. Therefore, she had to go bust and owe him a mighty eight thousand dollars in total. He readied himself.

The doorbell rang.

Jackson paused. O'Reilly looked at him.

"Who's that?" he said.

"Answer it, Jackson."

"I can't: I'm playing blackjack. She might cheat while I'm out of the room."

O'Reilly stood up, produced a gun from under her jacket, and checked that it was loaded.

"Okay," she said, "I'll go to the door: You sit there and play blackjack with the hostage."

And with that, she left the room. Jackson looked at Celine with a broad smile. He had seen a way to increase his winnings.

"Now, Miss Naville, are you sure you want to increase your bet before you take another hit?"

The lounge was separated from the entrance to the apartment by a narrow corridor some twelve feet in length. O'Reilly stole silently along the worn carpet, gun in her left hand, listening for any sound outside. But there was no sound, no knock, no footstep, no voice. She wondered who it might be. In the five months they had been here, they had rarely seen any of their neighbors and had exchanged no words. They had cultivated no friends. The mail was not delivered here and the landlord never called. She looked through the small spy-hole: no one there.

Robert waited beyond the door, hidden to one side. He hoped it would be O'Reilly, as he had no plan for getting past the greater physical obstacle of Jackson. Al had suggested waiting until daybreak, when a caller might arouse less suspicion than in the middle of the night.

It had then taken Robert two hours to find the apartment, hidden away at the center of a massive development where all signs, numbers, and names had been vandalized. All through the night, and with every delay in the morning, he had feared for Celine's safety and even now he hoped he was not too late. As the door was opened, he swung his fist around, not knowing with whom it would make contact.

* * *

Jackson turned the card. The ace of hearts.

Even as she felt the impact of Robert's fist on her face, O'Reilly was trying to work it out. There was something wrong here: This was the guy who did not requite. Why was he interfering? She fell back, stunned, as Robert rushed forward and pinned her left arm to the ground. The gun was torn from her grip and O'Reilly found herself staring down the barrel.

Jackson was also trying to work it out. Where did that ace of hearts come from? He had gone to such trouble to rig the deck. It wasn't fair. All his winnings wiped out in one unlucky break. Celine's obvious pleasure in this irritated him. He pulled the sweatband down over her eyes and put a line through his note of the score.

"Just as well we're not playing for real, huh?"

Jackson turned as the door behind him was kicked open. O'Reilly walked through with her good hand held against the left side of her face, obviously in pain. Behind her came Robert with the gun in his outstretched hand. Jackson leaped from his seat to hold O'Reilly, who appeared to be on the verge of collapse. Her cheekbone was sunken and swelling already.

"All right," said Robert to Jackson, "cut her free."

If Jackson had been calm and rational, he might

also have wondered why the nonrequitor was interfering. As it was, he was far more concerned with the injury to his partner. He was fed up with all this pain and injury. It would heal, but so what? People had to damn well learn to be more careful.

"What the hell did you do to her?"

"I punched her in the face."

Jackson lowered O'Reilly into a chair. "You punched her in the face? A woman half your weight and a lot more than twice your age and you punched her in the face? There was no call for that."

Robert had not expected this. He had done the difficult bit: getting inside, overpowering O'Reilly, and securing the gun. Surely they ought to just obey him now, not argue about his methods. The truth was that no, he didn't feel very good about punching O'Reilly in the face and in a perfect world it wouldn't have been necessary. But, as he knew only too well, this world was not perfect.

"She had a gun," he said.

Jackson was not to be fobbed off with such a risible excuse.

"She had a gun? Big deal. So that makes everything all right, does it?"

Robert, despite his determination not to, could feel himself being sucked into an unwinnable argument of excuse and damnation.

"I didn't say it makes it all right, I'm just trying to explain—for all I knew, she could have been a karate expert or something."

"With a broken arm? You ought to be ashamed of yourself."

This was too much for Robert. It reminded him of his schooldays when some wily teacher would dismantle his excuses for underachievement, one by one, until there was nothing left to blame but his own worthlessness as a human being.

"Okay," he shouted at Jackson, waving the gun towards him, "I'm sorry! Now cut her free."

As the tape was peeled from her mouth, Celine, still blindfolded, spoke her first words. "You bastard!"

"Celine—"

"What do you want? Come to rub salt in my wounds?"

"I've come here to explain."

Jackson pounced. His greater weight forced Robert to the floor. Jackson held Robert's wrist and smacked his hand on the floor until the gun was loosened from his grip. He tried to catch hold of it, but Robert pushed it away.

"What is there to explain?" Celine said, blind to the struggle at her feet. "Despite your crummy poem, I came to see you, and all you could do was humiliate me and turn me away. I thought you were decent, but it turns out you're just a lying, cheating bastard like all the rest."

Robert found it difficult to reply. With Jackson on his back, just breathing was a struggle.

"So go away and leave me alone."

Robert wriggled free momentarily.

"Celine, I didn't mean to hurt you. I don't know who wrote that poem, but those were my feelings."

"Oh sure," said Celine, as Robert's voice curtailed in a sharp yelp. Had she not been blindfolded, she would have seen that Jackson now held him in a headlock.

They both stumbled around the room as Jackson

tried to guide Robert's head into collision with a range of hard objects.

Behind the sweatband Celine was only aware of Robert's voice, moving around the room and punctuated by the sound of a skull in contact with wood, metal, and rigid plastic.

"When you left the diner last night—"

The door.

"—I realized that I had turned away the woman with whom I had spent the happiest, most exciting time of my life."

The fridge. A grunt of pain.

"—who means more to me than anything on this earth."

The television crashed to the floor, imploding.

"Remember that dream I had? I dreamt that my life was in danger, that my heart had stopped—"

The dull, solid thud of the oven door.

"—but you saved my life when you pierced my heart with an arrow, the arrow of your love."

Plaster crumbled from the cheap partition wall.

"And that's the truth."

There was a pause. Celine could hear the sound of both men breathing heavily. Robert's voice was weary. "What I'm saying, Celine, is that I love you."

Celine smiled, but before she could reply, she heard Jackson's excited voice.

"What did you just say? O'Reilly, did you hear that? What did you say?"

"I said"—Robert was confused by their interest—"what I said was—"

But he did not finish. They were all silenced and Celine detected fear.

"What is it?" she said. "What's happening?"

The reply came in a voice she did not expect, soothing and assured. "Don't worry, Miss Celine," said Mayhew, "everything's going to be just fine."

With the aid of vision Robert could see that Mayhew was quite plainly lying. He stood in the doorway with a silenced automatic pistol in his hand and murder in his eyes. He raised the gun and Robert blinked as two shots were fired. When he looked around, he saw that both Jackson and O'Reilly were dead, each shot through the center of the forehead. Mayhew glanced at them briefly and put the gun away.

Through the door behind him came another man, limping slightly with a stick to support him. It was Naville. He stared at Robert with the deep satisfaction of a predator who at long last has cornered his prey and intends that the slaughter should be painful and prolonged.

"Well," he said, "we're not just going to leave them here, are we?"

22

Robert sat in the back of the limousine, sandwiched between the corpses of Jackson and O'Reilly, each with their neat puncture wound. Behind him, in the trunk, he could hear Celine kicking and shouting. Naville had instructed Mayhew to place her there as punishment for her disrespect and transgressions against his paternal authority. Placing the bodies on either side of Robert was designed, successfully, to focus his thoughts upon his own possible demise. His survival, Naville had explained, was dependent on the return of the money. If only Robert would lead him to the suitcase, then all would be forgiven and he could walk away a free man.

Robert remembered his last sight of the precious dollars, floating en masse downriver toward one of the world's great oceans, but he decided to keep this memory to himself. Naville was a man who wanted solutions, not problems, and Robert worked hard to concoct a plausible answer.

"Now, Robert," said Naville, "I'm going to ask you one more time, and remember, your life depends upon this: Where is the money?"

"The cabin."

"Which cabin?"

"Where I held your daughter captive. I hid the money there."

Mayhew drew his gun again. "Where is it?" he asked.

"Kill me and you'll never know."

Mayhew snarled and replaced his gun.

As the miles passed by all too quickly, through town, suburbs, farmland, scrub, and hills, Robert went through his plan over and over again. The cabin was plausible: It made sense that he might have left the money there. Once at the cabin he would either break for the trees or attempt to overpower Mayhew with the aid of some heavy domestic implement. As far as he could tell, Mayhew looked solid, but beyond his prime. Still a good shot, though: Robert knew there would be no second chance. As they turned the sharp bend, the two bodies flopped onto him and he could see the butler gloating in the rearview mirror.

Naville sat opposite Robert, reveling in the young man's distress. He also looked at the two bodies: Mayhew had been right, it had been better to get rid of the two feckless bozos. Still, it was a pity about the woman, he'd kind of liked her. Now she was dead, he could study her face without any self-consciousness. Yes, she still reminded him of someone. The man, too. But who, where, or when he could not say. No one important, he decided, as the car lurched around a bend and O'Reilly's head slumped forward.

Rose Cedrice, agent 4033, was jolted from the article on "What Men Think You Think They Think" by the sound of the teleprinter. The afternoon shift in the communications center, deep in the bowels of the department, was usually a quiet one. Later on, she might expect a few prayers and perhaps a confession or two, which always provided some innocent amusement, but rarely were there any incoming signals so soon after lunch. She put down the magazine and tore the message from the printer. Unlike the prayers, it had been encoded and came to them via a long-term, earth-bound surveillance operative. She could not read the code, but that was not her job. She sealed the message in an envelope and set off up the hundreds of stairs and along the miles of corridors to deliver it to a man who could.

Gabriel was tired. His entire waking day, it seemed, was taken up with administration. Meetings, meetings, meetings, all day long. Budgets to cut. Staff to fire. Five-year plans. Ten-year plans. Millennial plans. And constantly he was fighting a rearguard action against the doubters, a loose coalition of vested interest groups who sought to remove love entirely from the domain of human choice and replace it with some sort of compulsory program. It was an important battle, but it wore him down, and lately he had feared defeat. All he needed, however, was one good case, one happy ending, just to shut them all up and prove the department's worth in a modern universe. But he had so little time to get involved in operational matters, he had almost no idea what was going on in the field anymore.

Of Jackson and O'Reilly's progress he knew very little. There had been occasional sightings, but nothing hopeful, nothing to suggest that they had finished and were coming home. He had mixed feelings about having sent them. On the one hand, they were his best shot, but if they failed, if he lost them, the effect on the department, in terms of both morale and manpower, would be catastrophic. They were key players, both widely respected, and sending them had been the final gamble: If it didn't pay off, he might as well clear his desk.

Agent 4033 knocked on his door. He had never seen her before, but this did not surprise him. These days most of his agents were strangers to him. She waited while he opened the envelope.

"Okay, agent, you can go."

"Is it important?"

Let her wait, thought Gabriel. It was a long time since he had read anything in this code, a mixture of Hebrew, Greek, Roman numerals, and small runic diagrams. Gabriel sighed and reached for his code book. Slowly he began to decipher the message.

It was not good. Jackson and O'Reilly had been sighted, but were noted to be out of operation and likely to be so for several months, pending recovery from serious head injuries. Their subjects had also been sighted, but the life expectancy of the male appeared to be short, and a beneficial outcome was thought unlikely.

Beneficial outcome, thought Gabriel, an observer's euphemism: no happy ending.

"It's bad?" said Rose.

"Worse than that."

"Jackson and O'Reilly?"

Gabriel said nothing.

"They are coming back, right?"

"No. No, I don't think they're going to make it back here. That's the rule, if things didn't work out."

"They didn't work out?"

"No."

Rose lowered her head and walked to the door. There, she turned again. "Isn't there anything you can do?"

"I don't have the authority to intervene."

She looked at him accusingly as if to say, You sent them, you sent our favorites away.

"Agent 4033, you can return to your post."

She slammed the door as she went, causing Gabriel to blink.

Locked inside the trunk of the limousine, Celine kicked at the metal panel and shouted again for help, but none came. Since they had not removed her blindfold, she had only been able to guess at what had taken place in the apartment. Jackson and O'Reilly, she presumed, were dead: She had heard two bodies fall to the floor after Mayhew's sinister reassurance. For one hideous moment she had thought that Robert might also be dead but, to her relief, she had heard Mayhew order him to "drag the meat" to the car. As she heard the second load being pulled across the floor, her father had addressed her for the first time.

"Celine, my dear, you disappoint me," he told her. "I lavish upon you the gifts of fatherly love and how do you repay me? With hurt and malice. I have worried so much about you in the hands of this creep, yet, when freed, do you return home? No. Where do you go for help? To your mother's, I presume, or how else do you account for the use of her car? And what happens? You are kidnapped. You see, my girl, this is what happens when you stray from my protection and authority. You must learn, Celine, you must learn."

As her father's footsteps faded away, she had become suddenly aware of the powerful arms of Mayhew lifting her and the chair as one unit. She screamed in vain as he carried her down the stairs and laid her on her side in a carpeted space that she knew from its smell and feel was the trunk of a car.

Her attempts to free herself had failed. She had achieved enough movement of her legs to kick, but her hands remained firmly bound. Now they had stopped and she heard them leave the car, dragging the bodies away. From the twisting ascent on the final stage of the journey, she had guessed where they might be going, although why, she had no idea. She had briefly resumed her attempt to attract help, but out here, she knew, there was no one to attract. She gave up and lay helpless and blindfolded in the dark, carpeted crypt, listening to the sound of birdsong.

* * *

A short distance away, inside the cabin, Naville was not thinking about his daughter. Her punishment would continue later. First of all there was the lesser matter of the young hoodlum to be disposed of. Naville sat at the table where Celine had declined to eat red meat, while Mayhew, armed and ready, barred the cabin's only door. Robert stood nervously in the center of the room, disappointed to see that the cabin held fewer escape routes than he had remembered. The windows all looked terribly far away, and standing in the doorway, Mayhew was a monolith of menace. The evidence for this quality was plain to see: Propped up on the seats beside Naville were Jackson and O'Reilly, their faces frozen in surprise.

Naville delivered a short speech in the manner of a prosecutor who enjoys his work. "So here we are then, the scene of the crime. Not your only crime, of course, merely one of many that you've committed against me. Let's recall, shall we? You invaded my office without an appointment, insulted me, assaulted me, damaged company property, stole a gun belonging to the company, stole my car, and, oh yes, shot me in the leg, kidnapped my daughter, and stole my money. Do you have anything to say for yourself?"

"I'll get your money."

"That's what I want to hear."

"I promise."

"So you told us. Now where?"

Robert looked around. As he tried to judge how many steps it would take him to reach a window he could leap through, he was aware of Mayhew's scrutiny and his finger on the trigger.

"Well?" said Naville.

"It's under the floor, sir," said Robert, dropping down and scraping at the planks of wood.

"If I could only remember which board it was. One of them was loose. I'm sure I'll find it. Just wait a moment." But none of the planks would come up. They were all held down firmly by thick nails and showed no signs of ever having been disturbed. Robert heard Mayhew sigh.

"Do you know, sir, I think he's bluffing. I don't think he's got your money."

"I think you may be right, Mayhew."

Mayhew stepped toward Robert, ready to bring it all to an end, but as his weight fell onto the next plank, it sank at one end and at the other rose half an inch above its neighbor.

"That's it," shouted Robert, "that's the one."

He wedged the tips of his fingers into the tiny gap and pulled desperately, wrenching the plank up. Able to get a good hold of the next plank, he tore this up as well. Now there was a big enough hole in the floor.

"It's down there, Mr. Naville, I'll just get it for you."

Naville and Mayhew exchanged indulgent looks, but agreed to let Robert have his moment of pointless hope. Robert did not notice—he was already lowering himself between the boards. Underneath the floor was a space about two feet high, surrounded on all sides by the low brick walls on which the cabin was founded. Robert looked around. The wall was all that stood between him and freedom, but it looked solid. Only at the front of the cabin, underneath the door, did two shafts of light shine through small faults in the brickwork. Robert crawled toward these, offering commentary for the men above him.

"I see it, Mr. Naville, I see it. I'm just going to get it. I just need to free it from the rubble down here."

He kicked at the wall. A brick came loose and he kicked again.

In the room above, Naville smiled and Mayhew shook his head as they listened to the wall being kicked away.

Looking around, Mayhew saw the ax with which Celine had experienced forced labor. He lifted it and weighed it in his hands: a nice, heavy blade. He stood in the doorway and rolled his shoulders a few times to warm up, then swung the ax with all his force.

The blade smashed through the wooden floor and stopped just in front of Robert's face. He recoiled. The ax was withdrawn and smashed through again, this time swinging lower and farther into the space. Beyond it, Robert had succeeded in creating a small hole in the wall, but now the ax blocked his escape. Even as he tried to work out a way past it, the ax began to approach him, smashing through the boards on either side, seeking to catch him in its destructive arc. He scurried back farther, but the ax kept on coming. He could hear Naville's voice.

"Face it, Robert, you don't have my money. But what you have to understand is that it's not the money that matters: It's the principle."

Robert was trapped in a corner now, as the floorboards splintered on either side of him. Suddenly a gap was torn open above and he could see Mayhew's red, sweaty face and the ax raised above his head for the final descent. Robert closed his eyes and heard Naville's voice deliver a cautionary rebuke.

"Mayhew, please. Not with the ax."

23

Gabriel smoothed his hair and fastened the top button of his shirt. He drummed his fingers on his desk and rehearsed again what he wanted to say. His plan was to be polite but firm, rational but un-yielding. It was not his habit, he would say, to make special pleas on behalf of either the department or individual operatives: They took the world as they found it and they did not complain, but the circumstances of the current case were of such complexity and the penalties for failure so great that he could no longer simply stand by and watch. Surely, he would conclude, if ever there was a time to demonstrate His power, that time was now.

Gabriel checked his watch. Was he phoning too early? Or too late? What would He be doing? Gabriel had never used this telephone before.

"Call me in exceptional circumstances" was the message he was given when he got the job, but never once in the history of time had he considered it necessary to do so. He had always been proud of both his and the department's ability to cope with any problem. Asking for help, he wondered, was that a sign of weakness or strength? He stood up and paced around, desperately hoping that some other option would present itself. He was aware of the scrutiny of operatives and agents standing in the office beyond his door, watching him through the glass panel. He could tell they were all willing him to make the call. Easy for them: It was his job on the line.

He picked up the phone, cleared his throat and dialed.

The voice that answered was that of a cherub "Hello."

Gabriel almost laughed. What a fool he'd been to think he might get through directly. This was only the switchboard.

"This is Gabriel. Get me God."

The telephone call did not last long. Gabriel stated his case, confidently at first, but with dwindling self-belief as he was aware of the ominous, deafening silence at the other end.

When he finished, there was a very long pause Gabriel dared not say more. He could sense every pair of eyes in the offices outside focused on him as he pressed the telephone to his ear and waited. He cursed himself. To try and then fail was a thousand times worse than not to have tried at all. Now he must endure a loss of face and authority so much worse than if he had stayed his ground. And Jackson and O'Reilly, what had he done to save them? Nothing.

The silence continued. Eventually words came. It was not a voice that spoke them and Gabriel could not even say whether he was hearing, feeling, or thinking them—they just came.

"Is that it?"

"Yes," replied Gabriel.

There was another, shorter pause, then more words. "Hmm, well, I'm afraid I don't think I can help you."

"Thank you, sir," said Gabriel. "Sorry, sir, I'm sorry to have bothered you. Sorry, sorry, sorry."

But the line had gone dead. Struggling to restore his dignity, Gabriel replaced the receiver and looked up to meet the stare of his audience. They looked away.

In another time and place, all times and all places, the Origin of the Word thought about the telephone call and Gabriel's plea for help. Strange request, it was felt. There had been no need for Gabriel to go into detail, for of Jackson and O'Reilly and Robert and Celine, all things were known. It was a case that had been watched with some interest and the outcome was awaited almost with excitement. But intervention, oh no, that was absolutely out of the question, contrary to every precedent that had been set. That was the great thing about earth and humans, the whole point: One never knew what was going to happen next. Still, it was possible to feel some sympathy for poor Gabriel, considering what he had to deal with. Love, you see was a strange and powerful child, accountable to no one.

Felix swallowed the last scraps of chicken and raised his big, doleful eyes to ask for more, but Tod had become worried about Felix's weight and decided to get tough on calories.

"No, Felix, you can't have no more."

Felix turned away.

"And there ain't no use in sulking. What good is sulking going to do?"

Felix shrugged.

"Exactly. None," said Tod, "and anyway, I think we have work to do, don't we?"

Felix barked once.

"Good. Now let's go."

They stood up and Tod looked once more through his binoculars. From his vantage point up the hill, he did indeed see everything. Today, as they sat down to lunch, he and Felix had watched a long limousine, the like of which they had never seen, arrive at the cabin beneath them. From this car had emerged two men, one of whom had a gun, and a third, none other than young Richie Vanderlow. Tod's first assumption that the two men were Richie's manager and bodyguard was eroded as he watched young Richie haul two corpses out of the car and into the cabin at gunpoint.

This was perplexing, but Tod had a possible explanation. After the karaoke, he had acquired a copy of *Rolling Stone* magazine in the hope of learning something about his new friend.

Of Richie there had been no mention, but there was a multitude of photographs of young men and women in bizarre situations. Was this, he wondered, one such situation? If so, however, where was the camera? His doubts increased when the sound of an ax splintering wood had begun to echo up the valley and Tod decided to investigate. Arming himself with a vintage flintlock pistol and a knife, he set off down the hill with Felix.

Knowing each inch of the terrain, and habitually fleet of foot across it, Tod and Felix reached the cabin in a matter of minutes. Tod's first instinct was to proceed directly to the cabin itself, but Felix was distracted and ran to the limousine, where he stood at the back, growling toward the trunk.

Tod, knowing Felix well enough to respect such actions, followed, and as he did so, Felix became increasingly excited, barking and trying to open the trunk. Tod tried also, but the trunk was locked. He nodded to Felix, who had lifted a heavy rock in both hands and now brought it down hard against the lock. Tod stepped forward and opened the trunk. This, he realized, was a serious situation. Inside, tied to a chair, with a blindfold around her eyes, was young Richie's wife, Lucille Vanderlow.

Jackson watched Mayhew pull Robert up through the hole in the floor. He wished that he could say or do something, but it was no use: His brain was just mush. Speech, movement, breathing, they were all gone. He couldn't even see or hear in the normal sense, but he knew what was happening and he knew that O'Reilly must feel the same. In a few days' time, perhaps, after some gruesome autopsy, their brains would begin to heal, but by then it would be too late because by then Robert would be dead. Jackson knew that if only he could move a finger or utter a single sound, Robert might have some chance of escape, but the scrambled egg inside his skull would not respond. Instead, he could only watch, helpless inside his corpse, while the execution drew nearer.

Mayhew held Robert in front of him, the gun at his head, while Naville stood opposite and delivered the final address. For him this was a moment of triumph, a timely reminder to the world that although his hair had turned gray with the passing of the years, Francis Naville's anger had lost none of its lustre. He was reasserting his ability to deal with a crisis, to smite his enemies and emerge victorious. In addition, there was a pleasing completeness about the day's events, all the issues were being dealt with at once: Robert, the two bozos, and Celine.

"So, Robert, you see, what happened was this: You shot them."

He pointed at the two corpses and stopped. It was O'Reilly. The light on her face, the tilt of her head: At last he had recognized her. But it didn't make any sense. A dance hall in the late sixties. *Are You Going to San Francisco?* He was dancing with an older woman who stood on his feet. He met the smile of a girl. Her partner was just as clumsy. Her name was Delilah and her partner was . . . Jackson.

But that was thirty years ago and they didn't look a day older.

"Sir."

It was Mayhew. Naville concentrated.

"Sorry. You shot them. These two, you killed them both, Robert."

He thought about the hospital. The doctor said she should have died. He was quite emphatic about it. But she didn't. Fell two hundred feet and smashed half the bones in her body.

"But she didn't die."

"Sorry, sir?"

"Are they dead, Mayhew?"

"Sir?"

"Are they dead, Mayhew? Are you sure they are dead?"

"I shot them myself, sir."

Naville looked at O'Reilly and down at her feet. It was her all right. The same damn shoes. He'd never forget those shoes. He could swear she was staring at him.

"Damn you."

O'Reilly wasn't staring. She couldn't. Her brain, like Jackson's, was mush. She sensed that Naville remembered her, but she didn't remember him. Perhaps they had met sometime in the sixties, she thought. She had met lots of men in the sixties. With the introduction of the free love policy, she and Jackson had been exceptionally busy during that decade, generating relationships at the rate of three or four a day, every day for months at a time. The program had been a disaster, of course. Perhaps Naville was one of its victims. If she could have spoken, she would have asked.

"Sir, shall we proceed?"

With difficulty, for his mind was full of bitterness and sentimental regret at the passing of his youth, Naville turned back to Robert.

"Right. Well, you shot them, and then you shot yourself. And then, while you bled to death, you set fire to this cabin, destroying all evidence. Didn't you?"

The door behind him was opened.

"Not yet he didn't." Celine was framed in the doorway, holding Tod's flintlock pistol with both hands.

Mayhew clutched Robert tightly in front of him as hostage and human shield.

"Celine, what are you doing here?" Robert said.

"Put the gun down," said Naville.

"Don't get in my way, Father."

"You're not in control of your actions, Celine." He approached her slowly. "You're unhinged. You need the most expensive psychiatric care that money can buy. So why don't you just give me that gun?"

He edged closer.

Celine looked not at her father nor at Mayhew, but at Robert. "Because your life is in danger, and as you dreamt, I shall save it with an arrow: the arrow of my love for you."

Naville gave up. The daughter was as crazy as the mother. He gave an order, crisp and unambiguous. "Kill him, Mayhew."

* * *

In another time and place, all times and all places, this event was watched and once again it was observed: strange and powerful child, accountable to no one.

24

There is no confusion in the records of Carsdale County Hospital. Everything is recorded exactly as it was in the initial clinical observations, the X rays, the operation record, and the subsequent progress notes made by the nursing staff, interns, and attending physicians.

Mayhew was shot through the upper chest on the left side, causing his left lung to collapse and a significant loss of blood. Following resuscitation in transit and on arrival, he was taken to the operating theater, where the hemorrhage was arrested and the injury repaired as far as was possible. His postoperative course was unremarkable and he was eventually discharged in good health to the custody of the state on two charges of murder, which he shared with his employer.

The records are equally clear about Richie Vanderlow (noted to be uninsured, but all costs met by wife). Despite his insistence that he had been shot, there was no evidence of any injury. A full physical examination was performed at the request of the patient, but he was discharged without any further investigation or treatment. In particular, his heart was considered to be functioning normally and in good health. The two small holes in his shirt, one at the front and one at the back, were of no interest to the doctor who examined him: Garment repair was not his trade.

Speaking of garments, no one bothered to look at the small fragment of bloodstained cloth that was picked from Mayhew's wound. Had they done so, they might have found that it matched the cloth of Robert's shirt, but the incinerator swallowed all waste and soon the fibers were nothing but smoke.

The police were equally uninterested in the young man's story. They had their own, much neater version of events. Robert had moved just as the flintlock was fired, saving his own life, and exposing Mayhew to the bullet which lodged, as described, in his chest. There was, they concluded, no other explanation and none required.

The entire investigation was conducted in this streamlined spirit under the close supervision of a homicide detective by the name of Gabriel. A care-worn, worldly man, he had explained to Robert and Celine that all he was interested in was a couple of quick convictions. In the circumstances leading up to that day, he had no interest.

"As I see it, it's like this," he told them, over coffee at the precinct. "Girl elopes with boy from wrong side of tracks after love-at-first-sight type situation. Father displeased with daughter and boy. Hires two desperadoes to retrieve and dispose respectively. Desperadoes very desperate and mucho unreliable. Kidnap daughter. Father and butler kill desperadoes and plan to kill boy and destroy all useful facts in fire. Plan thwarted when girl saves boy from certain death. No charges against girl or boy since acting in defense of life. Also no wish to complicate fast-track prosecution with extraneous detail of what is now history. For example, talk of possible involvement in bank robbery would simply allow defense to distract from prosecution case. Are we happy?"

They were happy.

Mayhew sang. Disgusted by his employer's failure to buy him free of all charges, he had decided that his bond of loyalty was severed. He knew where the bodies were buried, both literally and metaphorically, and did not shirk from describing exactly how, where, when, and why they had come to be there. By the time he had finished, the case against Naville was long and detailed.

Mayhew, however, was not saved by his own confession. In due course he was found guilty of several crimes, including murder, and he received, as expected, the death penalty. He launched no appeal and seemed to accept his fate with equanimity. On Death Row he was regarded as a model prisoner, passing his days in reading and in tapestry weaving. His request for a final meal, posted well in advance, was for roast beef, Yorkshire pudding, and a pint of warm bitter. When it was explained that alcohol was forbidden, he did not complain. As he showered in the mornings, they would hear him recite snatches of his favorite poetry.

> "It dawns in Asia, tombstones show
> And Shropshire names are read;
> And the Nile spills his overflow
> Beside the Severn's dead."

But on the morning of the execution, they opened the door of his cell to find that he had gone, simply vanished. The immediate activation of alarms, dogs, manhunts, roadblocks, and helicopter searches was all to no avail. Between being last observed through the spy-hole and the opening of the cell door, a period of only fifteen minutes, Mayhew had disappeared. There was no clue as to how he had effected such a security-defying escape, and the months of high-level inquiry that followed brought an answer no nearer.

He had left his cell in immaculate condition, not a speck of dust anywhere. His sheets were neatly folded. His few possessions he had taken with him and the only trace of his presence that remained was a small, handwoven Union Jack flag that flew from a stick on top of the table, fluttering in the draft of the air conditioning.

He was never seen again.

The prosecution of Naville did not founder for lack of evidence, since, thanks to Mayhew, of that there was a superabundance. The problem was that the defendant was judged, after a series of interviews by several psychiatrists, to be insane and unfit to plead. They all agreed that Naville had lost touch entirely with reality and lived in a world of obsession, delusion, and hallucination. Whoever came to see him, all they got was the same ritual gibberish, only becoming more and more embellished with detail as the months, and then the years, went by. His manner was that of a man who has a great secret that he tries to share with the world, but is driven to fury because the world will not listen.

"They are alive, you see? They're not like us. They don't die. You can ask my wife, my ex-wife. It was them, you see, in that dance hall. The same shoes, you understand, the same shoes. That's how I understood. Then I realized, she didn't die when she fell off the bridge: She can't die. You can check the records. It's all there. I paid the bill myself. A dollar is a dollar is a dollar. And Mayhew, yes, he shot them, but no, they're not dead. No, no, no. They were pretending. Laughing at us. And the bullet passed straight through him. I saw it happen. There was no mistake. He was an Aquarius and she's a Gemini. That's a highly adverse combination. Are you going to San Francisco? They're alive, you see, they're not like us. They don't die."

And over and over again he would repeat this cycle of thought. Often, as his listener departed, Naville would become desperate and violent and required restraint with powerful drugs.

Over time, he refined his theories and set them out in a treatise. Jackson and O'Reilly were immortal. They had orchestrated both his relationship with Delilah Benich (later Naville), and that of Celine with Robert. They were working for some celestial agency which made some such relationships its business and which sent them to earth to promote them. For the sake of clarity, Naville had decided to call this celestial agency "the Department." The

Department was a ruthless organization and its "operatives" (Naville's description) were obviously forbidden to leave earth until the relationship had begun. Thereafter, man and woman were on their own. Despite many hours of therapy, his faith in these theories only grew stronger.

Francis Naville never stood trial.

There were two objective witnesses who supported a certain aspect of both Naville's story and Robert's. Those witnesses were Tod and Felix, who had watched from just behind Celine as the bullet, they thought, passed through Robert's heart and into Mayhew. Unfortunately Felix's value as a witness was negligible, since he would only communicate with strange barking noises and had "not been the same since the war" according to all who knew him. As for Tod, his testimony was undermined by the damaging admission that he kept a barn full of human skulls and a scythe sharpened in readiness for Armageddon.

Their statements were never placed on file.

25
〰

The wedding took place about two months later, in a castle in Scotland. It was a simple affair attended only by the bride's mother and the groom's immediate family. All agreed that nothing could have been better, more beautiful or more moving than it was on that day.

Thereafter Robert and Celine spent a two-week honeymoon in the same castle and now, after dinner, they sat in front of a roaring log fire in the privacy of their apartment and discussed again the mysteries of life and love.

"So," said Celine, "you're telling me that successful relationships are made in heaven, not founded in the daily practicality of two people being prepared to tolerate each other's imperfections."

"It's not just 'successful relationships.' "

"Of course."

"It's love. And it comes from somewhere wonderful that we don't know about."

"And you reject the idea that love is emotional adaptation to physical necessity."

"Completely."

"I don't believe it."

"Fate intervenes in people's lives."

"In ours?"

"Yes. Fate brought us together and kept us together."

"Fate had a strange way of making its point."

"That's part of the beauty of it: It's a strange and powerful creation, accountable to no one."

"You nearly got killed."

"But I didn't. And here we are."

"Do you have any substantial evidence to support this?" said Celine.

"No," said Robert.

"It's absurd and irrational."

"I know that."

"Then why do you believe it?"

"Because, Celine, I'm a dreamer."

Celine thought this over. She watched the red sparks float up into the chimney. "Well," she said, "I guess that makes two of us."

They looked into each other's eyes and their lips met as surely as their souls.

"They looked into each other's eyes and their lips met as surely as their souls. The End."

Violet Eldred Gesteten read this conclusion with satisfaction. She had enjoyed this improbable love affair. It was late at night, but she did not worry: Her days of getting up early and going to work were gone forever. It was a pity, for in some ways she had enjoyed her role as Chief Supervisor (Hygiene and Cleansing) at Naville Industrial Holdings, especially those aspects which involved the savage imposition of tough conditions on those beneath her. But with Naville's departure, there had been a seismic shift in the corporate culture toward a more caring, sharing approach based on a fair assessment of each employee's abilities and needs. In this stifling, goody-two-shoes atmosphere, Ms. Gesteten knew that her time had passed. She was a carnivore surrounded by soft, slow-moving vegetarians, but forbidden to feed. Her resignation was soon tendered and accepted.

Much as she regretted the passing of this era, her life was not empty beyond it. Not at all, since for nearly a decade she had followed a dual career and now she was free to devote herself entirely to the second. Perhaps it was a move she should have made earlier, considering the success, the wealth, and the following that her alter-ego had already acquired. Certainly, this was the view of her agent, who had been pleading with her for years to "give up cleaning and start making some real money."

Well, so far the change had been a good one. She had more time and energy to devote to her craft, and her current project had been completed in near-record time. She issued a silent prayer that her readers would enjoy this tale of romance, drama, conflict, love lost and love found as much as they had enjoyed all her other efforts in the same genre. There was every reason to expect that they would. The key elements of boy and girl had not been disrupted. She thought about the title: *Perfect Love*. It was, she decided, perfect. She read the conclusion once more and then, beneath "The End," Violet El-dred Gesteten signed the manuscript, as she always did, with her *nom de plume* which was, of course, Virilia Consuela.

"Congratulations," Gabriel said, "you did it."

Jackson and O'Reilly acknowledged his praise, hard won and rarely given. But this had been no ordinary homecoming. From the moment of their return from earth, they had been feted as heroes, and on their arrival in the Department, the corridors had been lined by agents and operatives who cheered and applauded them all the way to Gabriel's office.

"I don't know how you did it"—Gabriel was smiling now—"and, to tell you the truth, I don't really want to know. But you did it."

Jackson and O'Reilly said nothing, their faces impassive.

"Guys, it was beautiful, it was practically art. Kidnapping the girl: That was a stroke of genius. A lot of operatives would have given up at that point—they'd have said, 'We've suffered enough,' but not you guys, oh no. I had faith in you, I knew you could do it and I knew you would."

"No problem," said Jackson.

"It was hard work," said O'Reilly.

"Hard work? I'll bet it was hard work. And I'm grateful, guys, I'm very grateful. You don't know what you've done for me, for everyone in the Department. You won a very important battle that you may not have known was taking place."

O'Reilly coughed. "Er, Gabriel, bearing in mind

all that you've said about what a big deal it was, and how hard we worked, and how everyone's so grateful and everything . . ."

"Yes, that's right, O'Reilly," said Gabriel.

"Well, we were . . ."

"What?"

"Well . . . weren't we, Jackson?"

"Yes."

"We were thinking of early retirement. With a pension."

"Vacation?" said Gabriel.

"No, retirement."

"I hear you, O'Reilly, vacation is really what you're asking for. Retirement would be a big mistake."

"We want to retire."

"Anyway, when you get back—"

"Back?"

"From vacation."

Gabriel threw O'Reilly a file which landed on her lap. "I thought you might like to take it with you. Read it on the beach."

"Oh, no."

"We can talk about it more when you get back: It's a tough case, but you'll crack it."

"Please, Gabriel."

"If I were you, I'd commence with the female."

John Hodge was born in Glasgow in 1964. He was never very good at games, but tried to compensate in later life by writing screenplays. *A Life Less Ordinary* (on which this novel is based) was the third of these, following *Shallow Grave* and the adaptation of *Trainspotting*.

GREAT MOVIE ACTION
FROM SIGNET

WINNER OF THE 1988
PULITZER PRIZE FOR FICTION
A MAIN SELECTION OF THE
BOOK-OF-THE-MONTH CLUB

BELOVED
TONI MORRISON

This profoundly affecting chronicle of slavery and its aftermath is Toni Morrison's greatest novel, a dazzling achievement, and the most spellbinding reading experience of the decade.

"A masterpiece . . . magnificent . . . astounding . . . overpowering"—*Newsweek*

"A brutally powerful, mexmerizing story . . . read it and tremble"—*People*

"A life-affirming novel . . . strong enough to break your heart."—*Boston Globe*